The Road to Kedarnath

Everyone is entitled to improbable gifts of grace

Dr. Immanual Joseph

Absolute Author Publishing House

The Road to Kedarnath

Copyright © 2022 by Dr. Immanual Joseph

Published by Absolute Author Publishing House

Contents

Foreword

This book is a quick read and a slow read. You can finish it under two hours, and you can read it for two years; you can read it once and you can read it time and again. This book has so many deep insights that I had to read it over and over. It encompasses a wide arc of human experiences: familial and personal relationships; material wealth and poverty; suffering and compassion; fear, rage and tenderness. In just over 160 pages the story takes you through guilt, pain and death while showing you how to overcome them.

It is hard to pigeonhole this book. This is a coming together of *The Prophet* and *Jonathan Livingston Seagull* – with a story of love and loss; death and rebirth thrown in – a masterpiece from an author who is waiting to be discovered by the larger population. It is a book for the long-term thinker – it will take someone years to comprehend the full meaning of some of the passages. The book will mean different things to different people and at different points of their life journey. And that is what makes a book timeless.

Immanual has drawn from centuries of wisdom and distilled it in a language that is readable and relatable for everyone. I have never visited Kedarnath, but the book took me on a pilgrimage while I sat in my home office; now I want to visit the place not just as a tourist but also as a seeker. The highlight of the book is how Immanual has managed to intertwine lessons from the Mahabharata and the story of the protagonists Arjuna and Krishna so seamlessly. You don't have to read the Mahabharata to enjoy the story and understand the lessons, but if you have, you will enjoy it no less.

I want to thank Immanual – a true seeker – for conveying his deep understanding of the complex nature of the world through this beautiful, timely and uplifting read. Finally, this is a book about love, written with love, and now surrendered to the world to find its own path. Just like the words in this book, *"The reward of love is the act of loving itself. When we love deeply, without expectations, without fear, we manifest God and God becomes us"*.

- Ferose V.R

Author of Gifted, Grit and The Invisible Majority

Founder India Inclusion Foundation

Senior Vice President at SAP

Dedication

I grew up in Chennai, India in a time before the internet and cable TV.

On lazy Sunday afternoons, I would lie down on my mother's lap, she would stroke my hair and tell me stories. She taught kindergarten, and storytelling was her specialty. Through songs and the spoken word, she led me through worlds of talking bees and errant kings, fables of adversity and triumph, and kindness that overcame all suffering in the end. Stories brought me happiness and hope. My mother's story sessions were the source of my learning and became the foundation of my moral compass.

Today, when her stories are dying out, I am grateful to be able to tell my own.

I hope that somewhere, someone will be made happier and hopeful by them.

This book is dedicated to my mother, a master storyteller, and to the healing power of stories.

News Flash

Pregnant Woman Killed in Car Crash near I-10

By Jennifer Steel, Staff Writer, Published November 23, 2007, AT 6:29 AM

A young woman and her unborn child were killed in the early hours of Black Friday morning when the car she was driving crashed into a wall on South Interstate 10 East Service road near Aurora Avenue on Thursday night.

According to Jefferson Parish Patrol, Alice Venkatraman, 26, was pronounced dead at the scene of the accident. Her husband Arjuna Venkatraman, 28, who was a passenger in the car was admitted to a hospital with non-life-threatening injuries. Witnesses claim that the Toyota Corolla being driven by the deceased suddenly veered off the highway into the service road before crashing against a wall. The impact instantly killed Mrs. Venkatraman who was seven months pregnant at the time. The couple was returning from Baton Rouge after spending Thanksgiving with the parents of the deceased.

Mrs. Venkatraman worked as an elementary school teacher at Gabriel's Elementary in Uptown New Orleans. She is survived by her husband, a software engineer, her parents James and Diane Blake of Baton Rouge, and two brothers. Jefferson Police are investigating the cause of the accident.

Chapter One

Arrival

Home.

Everything changes.

People, things, memories.

This airport from ten years ago. Grimy, noisy, disarrayed.

The airport has changed. It is still noisy, but it seems brighter, cleaner. People seem more courteous, more formal. Chennai is an international destination now.

Seven years is a long time.

Everything changes. Everybody changes.

Including me.

I step out, past the flimsy metal barricades and airconditioned corridors of the airport into a swirl of chaos. The intense humidity of my once-hometown blasts into my face, pungent with the acrid smell of exhaust fumes and tobacco smoke. A great mass throngs the airport premises, clawing into the realities of the night with memories, hopes, and dreams.

I am alone. There is no one at the airport to receive me. No one even knows that I am here. If they did, I doubt anyone would care.

It does not take long for the taxi drivers to sense that I do not have a ride. Suddenly there is a crowd milling around me, entreating, grabbing, cajoling me for my business. The most persistent of the lot has already grabbed my hand luggage. I meekly follow him to his taxi. Once I am inside his car and he senses a firmer bargaining ground, he gets ready to negotiate. I give him the address, he quotes a number, I nod my head. This is the address I grew up in- this was my home for 23 years until I left for America to pursue higher education. I hope my father still lives there.

Hope.

The driver- a young man with tired eyes tries to make small talk. He hurls his limited English vocabulary at me, hoping to impress himself. He realizes soon that his customer is lost in a different world. Perhaps he sees me tearing up in his rearview mirror. There is a genuine note of concern.

"Saar, everything okay saar?"

I turn away and look at the fleeting street lights. Memories begin to swell up- the good ones swallowed up by the bad ones.

'...*of all the things ever said and seen, the saddest are these, it could have been*'- a distant quote from a distant past from who knows where. For some reason now, those lines are clanging into my mind in pulsating rhythm.

Seven years have gone by since that last fateful phone call.

All that anger and ego seem meaningless now. But the years are gone. Only the scars remain.

"Saar, we are here."

I look outside through the open window of the taxi. Yes, this was my home- the traditional pyolled house with a green door and dirty cream-colored walls and a metal gate separating it from the street. But it seems so small now... shrunken and withered. The largesse of my childhood perception crumples to reality.

The taxi driver gets out of the car and unloads my two suitcases and handbag from the car trunk. He opens the door respectfully and waits for me to exit. I hesitate. I have dreaded and dreamed this very moment for so long now. Will my father recognize me? I have not bothered to check if he was alive or dead in all these years.

"Saar?"

"Some more time," I manage to whisper.

The driver closes the car door and sits down by the curb. He pulls out a beedi* and starts puffing contently on it.

I have come a long way home. This thought of reconciliation has given me hope and kept me sane through the grueling months past. I have nowhere else to go, no one else to meet. A perfect stranger in his own hometown.

This street. I used to play cricket with friends right where this taxi is parked. Burst crackers during Diwali. I was loved. I loved. Everything I loved I traded for another love. Memories.

I steel myself and step out of the car. Even the night seems noisy under the street lamps. A dog howling into the distant night, a roadside sleeper coughing and rustling under his blanket. I walk up to the metal gate, hesitate, and then push it open. There is a faint creak, but my heartbeat seems louder.

The taxi driver is behind me dragging my suitcases and handbag. We place the bags at the doorstep and the driver retreats to his taxi. I wait outside the green wooden doors of my house, hand raised, ready to knock, but not quite managing to do so. I sit down by the door- a pariah created out of guilt and pain. I weep.

The moon is bright.

The taxi driver is staring at me from across the street, puffing on a new beedi.

He is unsure of what to say or do.

I bury my head in my hands and sob for the things that could have been.

I don't know how much time has passed by. The driver is kneeling down by my side.

"Saar, I must go. Please settle my fare. It's already been an hour."

I look at the man.

He is thin. His cheekbones are jutting out. He is young. Probably a dream chaser. Like thousands of young men who come to the city seeking identities. Identities that the city and hunger have claimed.

"Are you married?" I ask him quietly.

He is obviously surprised.

"Yes, saar. My wife and kids are in the village."

I look at my house, the crumbling paint on the walls weaving pictures from my past. I walk outside the metal gate and close it gently. The suitcases, the handbag, the seven-year-old gifts. In the morning, when my father... or whoever is in that house now... opens the door, there will be some wondering to do.

"You want to go somewhere else saar?" the driver asks. He is confused, probably worried that I may not pay him for the extra time he has spent waiting for me.

"How old are your kids?"

"Seven, six, and three saar. All girls. Why do you ask?"

I reach out into my pockets and pull out my wallet. American dollars, credit cards, driver's license, everything. I give my wallet to the driver. He is confused...shocked.

"What? I..."

"I don't have any use for these anymore," I tell him. I am surprised at how calm my voice is.

"Saar....just give me my fare. I will go. I don't want trouble." He sounds panicked.

"Take your fare and throw the rest into the trash if you have to," I tell him and start walking away.

It feels good. I feel good after a very long time.

More coughing from the roadside sleeper. The moon is bright.

I look back when I turn the street corner. The driver is still where I left him. His head is bent trying to fathom the contents of my wallet in the moonlight.

I smile.

I feel free.

Chapter Two

Kedarnath

People come to Kedarnath to seek atonement.

Lord Shiva, who maintains the balance of the Universe through death and destruction, is honored with many names. Here, he is Kedarnath, the Lord of the Field -the field where the crop of liberation from the cycles of birth and rebirth grows.

As legends go, the Pandavas- five brothers who were cheated out of their rightful inheritance, fought a long and painful battle against their more powerful cousins. When they had killed their erring relatives and war was done, the Pandavas came to the Himalayas seeking Shiva, who had the power to absolve them of their sins. Shiva hid from them, taking the form of a bull and burying himself under the ground in these mountains. But the Pandavas found him and dug him out. Impressed by their dedication, it is said, Shiva absolved them of all their sins.

I am hoping that the God of this mountain will absolve me of my sins. For three years I have wandered the streets of India with my many identities- murderer, thief, madman, beggar, renunciate. I have come here to put my identities to rest. A cannabis-smoking sadhu (renunciate) sent me here with wishes that I will find the right place to kill myself.

I am seeking not only to escape from this life, but from rebirth.

The wise ones tell us that life is suffering. Just when you think you have done with the pain, you are born into the next cycle of life. What you do in this lifetime decides what you become in your next life. There is always a next life, there is always suffering. I know that the part about suffering at least is true.

When I arrive in Kedarnath in the last week of October, the temple has closed for winter.

I am not here to worship at Kedarnath. I am here to find Bhairav jhamp- the suicide spot which I was told would cut the umbilical cord that connects me to rebirth. I stand outside the closed temple doors and pray that the Gods that hold the rosters of rebirth would be kinder to me in my next life. I pray that the deafening clamor inside me would quieten down before the end.

Kedarnath is a small temple town in Garhwal Himalayas. The thousand-year-old temple is the heart of this town. For six months of the year, from May to October, devotees throng this place. Hundreds of thousands of them, seeking forgiveness for their sins, seeking hope. The buses stop a few miles down and the last few steep miles up are done on foot. Or donkeys. Donkeys that are drugged, overworked, half-dead from exhaustion so they can carry people to salvation. What they did in their previous lives to earn their fate in this lifetime, no one knows.

With the tourists, come the businesses. People from the many towns down below set up shop in the town- setting up makeshift shops in spring which they disassemble in winter. For six months, nature is forgotten in the human melee of survival and greed.

Then winter comes.

Winters in the Garhwal Himalayan mountains are harsh. The roads leading to Kedarnath become inaccessible. When the snow falls, it falls incessantly. So people leave, and take God with them to the town of Ukhimath in the valley below. Then the mountain covers herself in her cold blanket of snow, and goes to sleep.

I walk around the nearly empty streets of Kedarnath on this late afternoon. A handful of last-minute stragglers are leaving town. They see me and bow in reverence. I suddenly remember that I am dressed in the saffron garb of a renunciate. I play the part one more time- I raise my hands and mutter a prayer that they will find their prosperity. When they leave, I laugh. The blind leads the blind. I, the one without direction, am blessing strangers that they will find theirs. My friend, the crazed sadhu, had told me that if it was my destiny I would find the directions to Bhairav jhamp. How, I do not know.

Bhairav jhamp is not a tourist spot. There are no signboards pointing the way. A hundred years earlier, our colonial masters had outlawed the practice of suicide-to-escape-rebirth at Bhairav jhamp- and, as with many other things that suited their sensibilities, erased the history and the location of this spot from public memory.

I pull my woolen blanket tighter around my body, but the bitter cold claws into my skin. I turn into a small bylane near the temple. I see a tea shop. It is the only one where there is some movement. The tea shop too seems to be shutting down. I walk over.

A thin man with a long graying beard and sparkling eyes greets me at the door of the tea shop.

He smiles. Even in my chaotic state of mind, I realize there is something extraordinary about this man. For a moment, the seething waves inside quieten down.

I bow.

"Are you hungry?" he asks.

I have not been thinking about food, even though it has been a day and a half since I ate anything.

I see that his shop is already emptied out. The tea vessels are probably cleaned and packed. There is a bundle of possessions wrapped in tarpaulin material ready to be moved out.

I shake my head.

"It's okay," the man says kindly. "Sit here." he points to a stone slab by the tea shop. "I will find something."

"I am fine," I lie. "I am just looking for a place. Do you know where Bhairav jhamp is on this mountain?"

He stops smiling and looks deeply into my eyes. He muses for a while.

"I might. Why don't I get you something to eat first? You do look hungry!"

Against my insistence, he opens up the packing, rummages through and finds sliced bread, jam and butter, and makes me some sandwiches. I gobble them up quickly.

"Wish I would make you tea. Not to boast, but I have heard people say that my tea is the best in Kedarnath."

I thank him for his kindness and ask him again about Bhairav jhamp.

"Yes, Bhairav jhamp. It's on my way home. I will show it if you come with me."

I assume he is traveling down the mountain to the valley as everyone else.

"Is Bhairav jhamp on the way down to Gaurikund?" I ask

"No, it is on the way up, about an hour's walk from here."

He notices my confusion.

"Yes," he continues, ' I do not go down to the valley. I live in a cave up the mountains during winter. That is my home. The jhamp is on the way to my cave"

I am surprised.

"Doesn't it get very cold here in winter?"

"Oh yes, it does. But I have learned to adapt. There is a quiet and peace here that you cannot find anywhere else."

He looks at me keenly.

"You could do with some quiet and peace yourself don't you?"

He laughs. My intent is probably very obvious. After all, I am asking for directions to a place whose only distinction is being a suicide spot.

"I hope you liked the bread and jam. I can make you some more if you want."

"It was delicious," I reply. "Thank you. But I am full."

"Alright then. Let me pack up and put away whatever needs to be put away for winter. Then we can leave."

He gets busy, taking down the last of what is in his tea shop and wrapping them in tarp, and moving them to an inner room. He chats happily as he works.

"I did not ask for your name?"

"Arjuna" I reply.

"Arjuna, I am Krishna." He pauses for a moment, then smiles. "The warrior and the charioteer meet here in these mountains."

He is referring to Bhagavad Gita. Arjuna, the Pandava prince is facing a moral dilemma about war. Krishna, the eternal living soul, now in the form of a charioteer, becomes his counsel. Krishna advises Arjuna to uphold truth through selfless action. And 700 verses of profound wisdom are created for eternity.

Krishna is pointing to the similarities of names between us and the protagonists of the Bhagavad Gita.

The belongings are bundled up again, last-minute cleanups are done and the shop is shuttered. Krishna tried to lift his heavy bundle onto his back. I offer to help.

"It's okay," he says, "I am used to this. Every two weeks, during summer when I am here at the tea shop, I go back to my cave to clean it up and stock food for winter. I have walked this path a thousand times over many years."

"Yes, but I can at least show my gratitude for the bread and jam by carrying your burden up the mountain for you ...until I reach my destination."

Krishna smiles and accepts.

The paved paths end very quickly. After that, we make our own. But Krishna knows every stone and scraggly patch of grass that leads upward. He tells me that this is the easiest path up. I am surprised to see his agility.

The burden is heavy and I am glad when we come to a stop by a flat expanse of rock overlooking a great chasm below.

"This is the place. This is Bhairav jhamp."

I unload the bundle from my back and peep over the edge. A tiny pebble loosens off the ground and into the chasm and disappears without a sound.

So this is it!

This is how I will go.

I want to sit and reflect on my life one last time, pray for forgiveness before I make the final jump.

"Thank you for showing me the way," I turn to the older man, who is looking at me with kind eyes. "You must go on..."

But Krishna doesn't go.

He plops on the ground.

He asks me to sit down next to him.

"Look, Arjuna. I don't know your story," he says patiently. 'I don't know where you come from and why you want to end your life. But I can tell you one thing... whatever stories you are carrying with you, there is a better way of looking at them. The decisions that you make in your darkest moments are almost always wrong.'

This stranger, his voice is compassionate, his eyes are gentle. On this cold evening filled with darkness inside and out, this man comes to me like a ray of light.

"I cannot tell you what you should or should not be doing. You probably have a million reasons to have come to this point in your life. But life sends people into our lives to remind us that there is hope. I am sure there are alternate points of view to your suffering. I know that even the darkest clouds will lift and the sun will shine through in time."

"There is too much pain," I reply. "I have done terrible things with my life, hurt people, the ones that loved me the most. Again and again and again, I have made choices that have placed me and others in pain. I am seeking release not only from this life, but also from more lifetimes of this suffering."

Krishna is silent for a while.

"Do you want to know a secret about Bhairav jhamp? There is nothing miraculous about this place. This rock on which you stand is a rock, it is a part of the mountain like that rock over there and this one over here. Every bit of the mountain is a miracle in its own right, but not in a way that it will break you away from cycles of rebirth and suffering."

He chucks a tiny pebble into the chasm from where he is sitting and continues.

"Listen Arjuna, I do not know if there is life after this body dies. I cannot talk about places I have never been to. All I know is that I am here, now, in this moment, talking to you, a stranger to me until this afternoon, hoping you won't jump off this mountain. The one thing you cannot do is go back to the past and undo what you have already done. You say you have made bad choices. Why add one more to it?"

I had no other thought except suicide in my mind when I took the journey from Varanasi to here. There is something about this man- his voice and his presence- that is shaking me out of my stupor.

"Arjuna, I live alone in the mountains. What I miss during the long cold winter days is a good story. Come with me to my cave. It is not far from here. Tell me your story. I will listen. And perhaps I can share something that you will find useful. And if in the end, you still need to seek out the path to absolution in the way you have chosen now, Bhairava jhamp is not too far away."

Miracles are when the heart moves and the mind cannot comprehend.

Krishna, I realize, is a miracle maker.

We sit silently on the ledge while the sun begins to set.

"But what about the food and clothing... " I wonder out loud. "I do not have anything. I could go back down the way I came."

Krishna shakes his head.

He does not seem as surprised as I am about the speed with which my heart is shifting.

"There are many paths you will see on your way, Arjuna. None of them were placed in front of you by accident. I believe you and I are here, having this conversation for a reason. I can sense, that the universe has placed us here in this moment because we need each other. And don't worry about the logistics. We will find a way."

He gets up, smiles at me, and loads the bundle on his back.

"Come," he tells me gently. As uncertain as I am about putting off my goal for another day, I get up and begin to follow him.

I feel safe, as I would have in my mother's presence. I have not felt this way in a long time.

"Just a little bit further and we will be home. You know, we can dread the adventure and make misery of it. Or we can embrace the adventure and live to tell a tale. Let's make this a winter of tales, Arjuna."

Chapter Three

Krishna's Cave

Our collective consciousness flows like a river.

Its banks are time.

Origins forgotten,

it carries stories and hurts of the past

digs up drama and dreams in the present

barrels toward the unknown with hope.

We, tiny drops of that river

tumble along with the writhing masses for a while

shaped and reshaped by the experiences of our time

Each of us clinging to the silt of the past,

digging up drama in the now

Wailing, laughing, Hurting, Healing.

We write our own stories

And make ourselves the heroes of this play.

Once in a while,

a drop of that river becomes aware and realizes that it does not have to be the river,

that it has no attachment to the silt from the past or the drama of the present.

Its hopes are not the hopes of the river.

And in a leap of awareness and mindless courage

it splashes out of the river

Toward the searing sun

and becomes cloud

From its vantage view, it sees the struggles and hopes of the surging waters

It witnesses laughter and tears,

It remembers but remains unfettered.

Krishna is a drop of the river that chose to become a cloud.

It has been two weeks since I came to stay with Krishna in his cave. I have not gone back to Bhairav jhamp.

The cave is a little distance interior to a cliff face. The narrow entrance leads to a small grotto and then into a rather large room. This is where Krishna and I sleep. He has shared his clothes and blankets with me. We sleep on the floor on folded blankets, our sleeping spaces separated by a tiny fireplace in the middle. Krishna has created a larger fireplace in the grotto. This is where we cook our food. We close the entrance to the cave with a door of branches and boughs woven together with rope. This keeps out the wind and snow on cold windy nights. When it is a little warm, we move the door and sit by the fire in the grotto, and talk.

Most evenings, I find Krishna looking away dreamily past the mouth of the cave, sipping on his tea. The clouds float quietly over the deep gorge outside the cave, engulfing us in a shawl of gray. Sometimes the sun peeps through the clouds in a brilliant effervescence of silver and gold. The steaming tea is a perfect antidote to the monotony of the cold evenings. Making and drinking tea is one of Krishna's greatest pleasures. It is a routine that he never misses.

Making tea in the mountains requires planning. On rainy days Krishna leaves a clean vessel out in the open to collect water. When there is no rain, we collect fresh snow. He filters the water and then sets it on a rolling boil on the metal tripod over the fireplace. It is soothing to watch him make tea. The tea powder and masalas are arranged in little airtight containers that he stocks on a little protrusion on the cave wall, along with salt and condiments. He carefully measures out the tea powder in tiny spoonfuls, empties it into the boiling water, and gently taps the spoon on the edge of the pot. He grinds the cardamom, cloves, cinnamon, and dry ginger in a tiny mortar and pestle, and carefully adds the masala in pinches to the boiling tea. Every action is deliberate, artful, an act of love. Somedays,

when he feels up to it, he uses condensed milk and brings
out the biscuits. If I had not been tagging along, he probably
would have had condensed milk and biscuits every day.
Since I am here, we now have to ration the cans, just
as we ration all other food- rice, pulses, pickles, even
the sewn-leaf plates we use for eating food. But Krishna
does not complain. He goes about his days with absolute
contentment- calmly and deliberately- a half-smile on his
face. He does not at all seem bothered that I have invaded
his personal winter haven and I am using up his resources.

In the inner room of the cave, there is a pile of Krishna's
stuff wrapped in plastic.

Krishna rummages through the pile for additional blankets.

He pulls out an old-fashioned tape recorder from
somewhere under the heap along with a plastic bag full of
cassette tapes.

He smiles as he shows this to me.

"Some of these tapes have old Hindi songs," he tells me. "I
don't know which ones. Unfortunately, I overwrote most of
these tapes with my own ramblings. You can use this if you
want- if you want to listen to songs or at some point, you
feel like you want to record your own thoughts and play
them back."

"Thank you. But I cannot imagine recording over what you
have recorded."

He laughs.

"It really doesn't matter, Arjuna," he assures me. "When I bought this cassette player years ago, I thought it would bring me comfort to listen to songs from my past. These are songs that evoke in me memories of my childhood. But sometimes, even memories can feel like prisons. I get a lot of time for reflection here. So as ideas came up, I started recording them over the songs. I felt proud of my thoughts for a while. Then, one day, it struck me. There is nothing that I was sharing that has not already been said. I realized there is more truth and wisdom in silence. So I bundled up my cassettes and put them under the tarp. I am learning now how to listen to the voices of silence."

I receive the player and bags of cassettes and batteries from Krishna. The cassettes are old. Most are soundtracks of Hindi movies from the 1960s and 70s. Krishna has scribbled on their inner pads in Hindi- thin gnarly ballpen words that are hardly legible. There are cassettes labeled 'Acceptance', 'Peace', 'Seeking', and some which I cannot decipher.

I am curious to learn what lessons these cassettes have for me.

When the snow muffles the sounds of the day, thoughts grow louder and louder.

Krishna's tapes have become my reprieve from the clamor inside. There are only a few batteries, so I am careful to ration my cassette time. But as I listen to his recordings I try to commit the essence of his words to memory so I can reflect on them in the endless silence of this winter- like a cow chewing mental cud. I remember hearing that the answers are always available for those who have the right questions. Whenever my heart is troubled, I reach out to a random tape and play it at whichever place it has stopped at. As wild as my approach is, the universe seems to send me that which I need to hear most.

I have stopped questioning the ways of the universe.

Chapter Four

An Old Man Dies

*R*arely do doors slam shut.

The door inches to the jamb and is ignored.

The light still comes through.

But slowly and surely the door inches forward

A little less light every day

And still no one notices

Until one day the door seals the pathway

and no more light comes through

The dark becomes our place

The dark becomes our soul.

Soon we forget that open doors exist

and that light shone through them.

Indra, the king of Gods, is cursed by his own guru to become a pig. Indra, the pig, wallows in the dirt, eats filth,

makes pig-love, has piglets. Brahma comes searching for
Indra to take him back to heaven. But Indra, having lived
the life of the pig, sees no greater heaven than the mud
and filth he has learned to wallow in. Ambrosia and apsaras
are now figments of imagination for him. His life with his
family, pigs though they are, is tangible, enough. He refuses
to return. Only when the gods of heaven kill his family and
his physical body, is Indra released from the illusion of his
pig-self.

Money seems to serve one fundamental purpose. It is to
shield humans from true human nature. And true human
nature is neither good nor bad- it is one of opportunism.
When a human is presented with opportunities for
survival and safety, he will take them. Values, beliefs,
and accompanying stories will be accommodated to his
choice of survival and safety. Money represents survival
and safety. Consequently, all higher intent is modified to
accommodate money. When all needs for survival and
safety are met, money loses its charm, because people
become equals. Money is not evil per se, but it is indeed a
cruel henchman.

I remember the first time I experience real hunger.

After I discard everything I owned into the garbage in
the early hours of that morning, I walk without stopping,
almost running, to distance myself from the horrid guilt

that was tormenting me. As I walk, the city wakes up, the screen doors of its morning part, and a throng of humanity rushes into the day. Amidst the smothering clamor and smells, I stand alone- a lost human without a destination in a city of 7 million rushing towards theirs.

It is late in the afternoon before another sensation begins to compete with the turmoil inside. This one comes from the pits of my stomach. I realize I haven't eaten anything since my flight meal. I am suddenly weary. I sit on a stone bench by a roadside coffee shop. It hits me that I have no money, absolutely nothing. I feel naked, helpless, although of my own making.

Just then someone steps in front of me.

It is a beggar. He is a middle-aged man with a tin can. He shakes his tin can in front of me. It rattles with coins. I have nothing to give him. I tell him so. I tell him I am hungry. We are equals now. He laughs and walks away.

But he comes back in a while.

This time he has some buns and two cups of coffee. We sit there silently, eating buns and drinking coffee- two beggars made equal in the absence of money.

It is probably about two months after my return to India. I am not keeping track. I have wandered the streets, slept on the roadsides, eaten scraps and handouts. A part of me constantly reminds me that this suffering is optional and that there is a way out. A larger voice inside though is resisting- urging me to self-flagellate for the unforgivable crimes I have committed. But most of my days are blurry. The inevitable shocks of vagrancy on the merciless streets awaken me from my leaden state every now and then. Hunger forces me to wake up and seek food. I find that people, especially the small streetside shop owners, are inevitably generous with food. I guess they too have experienced hunger and can empathize.

The very act of seeking is a welcome break from the apathy that is sucking me in. For me, everything has become a chore. Nothing has meaning anymore. The cruelty I am inflicting on myself seems better than the horrors that spawn inside. Without self-care, my personal hygiene and appearance have taken a nosedive. Layers of dirt cake my unwashed face and body. My clothes are soiled and tattered. I know my hair and beard are matted. Boils and sores are beginning to show up on my body, and I do not even care.

I am now one of the countless madmen and women on the streets of India. But most of the mad ones don't know that they are mad. Nor are they called so. Only those whose flavor of madness is different from the majority carry the labels of madness. Carrying the label of madness gives me a front-row seat to unvarnished human nature. I get a vantage view of human madness because of my newfound label. I think people are comfortable being themselves in front of madmen. Perhaps they know their own insanity will not be judged.

I remember, a long time ago, there was a destitute mentally-ill man, who we often found sleeping outside my elementary school. Disheveled, dirty, clothes torn-he fascinated and scared me. Perhaps because he was so different from me, I gave myself permission to be cruel. The boys and I would throw twigs or small pebbles at this sleeping man, laugh, and run away screaming when he awoke. This man must have had a story- a life of laughter and sorrow that somehow led him to the shade of a banyan tree outside an elementary school, to be mocked at and stoned by little children. If I had known his story, perhaps I would have been kinder to him.

Today, *I* am the mad man- disheveled and dirty, with torn clothes.

I am the one that children mock and throw stones at outside elementary schools.

How quickly the tables turn!

It does not take very long for me to experience the reeking realities of life as a beggar on the roadside. The physical challenges and uncertainties are only a small part of the pain. Here in the streets, I come face to face with the darkness of human nature, the one that crawls out into the open when people encounter others who have nothing to give them.

To the majority of people rushing through their days with grim determination to the great nowhere, I am invisible. In my current mindset that does not bother me. But there are some who are possessed by monsters- monsters that find validation by inflicting pain on those that cannot fight back.

I wake up with searing pain in my ribcage.

A policeman is towering over my crumpled frame, his hard-capped shoe raised to deliver yet another kick.

He needs no reason or excuse. He could have vented out his frustration on a tree. But the tree does not show pain. He wants to experience the fleeting whiff of power that happens by meting out pain to the ones down the ladder. A beggar sleeping on the roadside is certainly the lowest on the ladder, as far as human hierarchies go.

Thwump!

The sickening crash of the boot against an empty stomach

I reel in pain

A scream involuntarily escapes my mouth

It makes the policeman happy. He is possibly a constable, the lowest rung of his chosen profession. He has probably been meted out pain by the one above him, who in turn has received pain from the one above. He is simply a conduit of pain- passing it on. I fold my hands in obeisance, begging for mercy, curled in a fetal position.

He takes his wooden lathi and crashes it on my head, and I scream some more. A street dog that was sleeping a little distance away yelps and runs away. I had shared my food with him last night. He barks at the policeman from a safe distance. The policeman has a new object of domination- something more alive than this whimpering unresisting human crawling on the floor. He picks up a rock and throws it at the dog. The dog dodges. He barks more loudly. A bunch of other dogs join in. They surround the policeman. He picks up more rocks to throw at them.

He will not be outdone by dogs. After all, he is the superior species.

I crawl into the shadows behind a cement garbage bin, every inch of my body on fire from the pain, trailing blood and vomit.

People come out of their huts awakened by the clamor.

Someone yells at the policeman.

A screaming match starts.

The dogs continue to bark. I am forgotten in the melee.

Dogs have a remarkable way of showing gratitude.

I remind myself to feed more dogs.

And not to sleep in the open.

After all, one has to stay safe from the protectors of the land.

I am lying under a tree in some small town.

Someone is shaking me.

"Hey, you! Get up!"

I open my eyes. She is a middle-aged woman with a strong jawline.

"Have you had anything to eat today?"

She makes elaborate hand gestures to make sure I understand.

I nod my head.

"What is your name?" she asks me

I do not reply.

"You cannot talk?"

I remain silent. I just want to close my eyes and sleep.

"Come with me," she insists. "I will get you something to eat."

I nod my head in refusal and close my eyes. She talks some more and leaves when I do not respond.

A while later, a van stops by where I am lying down. I read the words on the van. It is from a mental health NGO. Two men come and cajole me to come with them. I protest. I ask them to leave me alone. They are strong. I cannot run away. Soon, I am in the van headed to my new home- the local mental health institution.

Several days go by in the mental health home. It is a busy place. The minute I arrived I was given a bath, shorn and deloused, and dressed in loose gray pull-up pants and shirt. I somehow do not want to talk about my identity. The institution seems to me a prison. I just want to escape back into the streets.

Matrons wander the halls where we are placed in. There are rows upon rows of beds on the ground. I am assigned to one in a corner of the hall. The doctors ask me many questions which I refuse to answer. Along with food, I am given sedatives. I sleep a lot. Sleeping feels good.

An old man sleeps on the bed next to me.

He is a rescue from the streets, like myself.

He does not talk, refuses to eat. He just lies there vacantly staring at the ceiling.

I overhear a matron telling a new doctor that the old man is a mentally ill destitute who was found eating his own human waste on a roadside. Possibly someone's parent, discarded when he became too much of a burden to be cared for at home. The old man is deteriorating, the matron informs the doctor. She says he may not be around too long.

Early in the night, the old man wakes me up with his coughing.

In the dim light of the hall, I see this man spasm with every breath. Even as I am lost in my own pain, I instinctively realize that this old man needs someone. I scoot over to his bed and raise his head onto my lap to ease his airway. The coughing subsides a little bit. The old man's eyes are, for the first time I have seen him, tracking movement. He is looking keenly into my eyes, his eyes glowing with memories of a long-lost life.

"Ramu," he calls me tenderly, "Ramu, why did you leave me like this?"

Clearly, he is hallucinating. He believes that I am Ramu. Who Ramu is to him I do not know.

"I am here now. Don't worry. Everything is going to be okay." I say tenderly

A gentle warmth eases into those scared eyes.

"Don't leave me Ramu. I am not angry with you."

The old man closes his eyes with a soft sigh. His breathing eases. His head is still on my lap. I stay like that through the night.

In the morning this old man stops breathing.

I realize I do not even know his name.

Two days later I find the big metal gate to the street open. I take the opportunity to slip out. Once again, I am a mendicant, wilfully wandering through the chaos.

All through our journeys, life offers us opportunities for redemption. If I had stayed there at the institution, I may have accepted help and come out of the dark inner space I was in. But I chose to leave, and that too was a choice of madness.

Chapter Five

Reflections In The Cave: On comparison

In my space of half-dreaming today, I visited a past of perfect choices.

In that dreaming, Alice and I and our daughter were living the beautiful life. My parents had reconciled with us. Our careers were flourishing. Everywhere I turned there was peace and hope...But the bitter cold shivered me out of my fevered longings and my heart pained with the dark ravishing of regrets.

I think of all the things that could have been. Different choices that could have led to different futures, and not the one I have landed myself in.

And it had become a morning of 'what ifs'.

I randomly pull out a cassette from Krishna's collection, load it into the cassette player and press the worn-out play button.

Krishna's voice is gentle and unhurried.

'How fleeting we are, how little we own, yet how much sorrow we carry!

How often we forget to simply be and let life be!

How much drama we concoct in our own tiny minds, how often we strive to live the lives of others forgetting our own!

How scared we are to ask questions that really matter, because we are afraid of the answers that may follow?

Trees that we are, we keep our roots shallow, because we think we can outrun storms

But the storms come fast and the storms come hard. And because of our shallow roots, easily we fall.

What instead if we start by seeking to understand our true nature?

What if we can look at ourselves unvarnished by made-up stories and untarnished by ego?

What if we can stop becoming distracted by all the shiny baubles that others carry?

What if we can end the relentless chasing and untangle ourselves from illusions?

What if we learn not to place our self-worth upon the shortcomings of others?

What if we open ourselves to the truth and allow the universe to take us on a ride and learn to sit back and enjoy the blossoming of life minute by minute, without agenda, without fear?

What if we can remember to gaze at life with wonderment in the knowing that we will not pass this way again.?

How little we need if we live only in this moment.

If we take away comparison, if we take away fear of the future, if we take away greed- we realize we can live on very little. What would have seemed traumatic circumstances become liveable when we learn to stop fighting and start accepting. The ones who experience pain are the ones who live in multiple worlds. They live in a reality they cannot accept and that reality becomes hell. They dream of other worlds where they would rather be. They dream of living the lives of others they see. Jealousy happens because they think of all the things that you could have been. It reminds them of missed opportunities. It reminds them of their own ticking clock. Straddling between desire and reality, they suffer.'

My eyes are closed as I listen to Krishna's musings.

I am a sponge soaking in as much of the wisdom spilling out of these tapes as I can.

I notice how I had started my mornings with what-ifs, and ending with what-ifs.

But how different the questions!

Chapter Six

Fathers

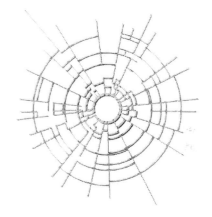

I remember a quiet afternoon from my childhood. Nothing remarkable about this one- no remarkable backdrops or backstories. It is a hot sunny South Indian afternoon- blazing heat that burns your feet when you step barefoot on the ground. Mom and I were returning from somewhere and we stopped at a temple. All the floors and structures are of rough granite. My mom rests under a temple structure, a handwoven plastic bag by her side. I am bored, full of energy. I am running around in my rubber sandals, oblivious to the heat, ignoring my mother's pleas. The hot afternoon air rustles up the sand near the granite, and other than the occasional gentle whooshes the wind creates, there is only silence. My mind is alive, open. There is no past or present at that moment. Even the dried-up peepal leaf of the sand is a delight. The temple is supposed to be a holy place, yet at that moment there is nothing holier than what is inside me.

An afternoon like thousands of others before and after- but this little ball of memory has chosen to stay. I do not know why. I feel warmth as I think about it.

Today, for some reason, we are discussing our Fathers.

Krishna and I are sipping tea by the fireside on a rainy evening, as has become our routine.

Whatever the trigger, I am thinking about my childhood.

Krishna seems to read my thoughts.

"Tell me about your father Arjuna," he says softly.

It is a hard topic for me.

I have never had a happy relationship with my father.

I knew he was essentially a good man- he worked hard in his clerical role, he never smoked or drank, provided for his family, and was never unfaithful to my mother. But he was hard- hard on me, his only child, and my mother. I can only remember him as a surly childhood presence, who smiled little and growled a lot. He had an inflexible ego about manhood and parenting, which he had inherited from his own father, that made him do things that I believe were contrary to his real nature.

I remember, when I was about 9 years old, I wanted to own a betta fish. One of my best friends had a few and was willing to give me one. But I needed my parent's permission. So I begged and pleaded with my mother. My mother, who by herself, had no concrete preferences and too scared to stand up against her husband, simply said that she was ok with it if my father was okay with it. I guess she had fought too many losing battles against his ego, and she did not want to add one more to her list. She added the caveat that if I study hard and get one of the top 5 ranks in the half-yearly exam, my father would most likely consent. So, that year I studied harder than I had ever studied. Even my father, who would call me a lazy bone at every opportunity he got, was surprised at my diligence.

When the half-yearly exam — came out in January, I was pleasantly surprised to see that my hard work had paid off. I had ranked 4th in a class of about 50 students. In all the prior years I had never scored better than the 10th rank. That evening, brimming with confidence, I picked up the betta fish from my friend in an old Horlicks bottle, and a supply of fish food. Coming home, I placed it on my study table, spent an hour admiring it, and then went out to play, When I returned home, I ran straight back to my study desk. My betta fish was not there. I rushed to my mother. She seemed very upset. She simply said I should have gotten my father's permission before bringing home the fish. I remember how my stomach curled when she said that.

"Where is my fish?" I screamed.

"Your father threw it away... it's in the garden."

I ran to the garden.

The Horlicks bottle was carelessly tossed under the banana tree. The fish was on the ground, the beautiful tail whose shimmer I had been admiring an hour ago, now surrendered to death.

My father had gone to the house of a friend to relax for the evening. I was livid with anger and hurt. I at least wanted my father to explain why he had done this to my fish. I wanted him to ask for my forgiveness.

When my father came back late that night, my mother told him that he was wrong to have hurt me like that. I remember them arguing. Soon after my father came into my room and gave me a tight slap.

"Next time be respectful to your father. Do you understand?"

He yelled. And then he stormed off.

I never had pets in my life ever again.

I share this memory with Krishna.

He listens, nodding his head solemnly.

"This meaningless stubborn ego of my father is what caused all of the misery I am in," I say remorsefully.

"Why do you say that?"

"All my life, my father tried to control every decision I made- from the clothes I wore to the college and branch of engineering I studied, and even the decision to go to America. If it was not his choice, my father believed it to be wrong. My conversations with him were always limited. While my mother often sided with me in private, she never, in all her years, put her foot down to support me in front of my father.

As a consequence, when I fell in love with Alice and decided to marry her, I was afraid to tell my parents. I was an adult at this time. Twenty-six years old, employed and financially independent, and free to do anything I wanted. But an invisible rope was holding me back. I guess, deep inside I knew I would not get my father's acceptance.

Alice and I married without informing my parents. Alice's parents were respectful of her decisions. So the marriage, which was held in a church, saw only her side of the family and some of my friends in attendance. When I said my wedding vows to Alice, I knew that a line had been crossed with my parents.

It was not long after the wedding that a friend shared a picture of our wedding on social media. The picture reached my parents.

I remember that night vividly when my mother called me. Alice was in the bed with me.

My mother was crying uncontrollably. She was yelling. How could I do this to them- their only son- to marry without their knowledge- to a girl of a different race and caste- of a different religion? How could I be so ungrateful, so cruel? What kind of a wicked sorceress she must be to trap their son in her web?

Her tirade went on and on.

I was seething with anger and hurt at her unguarded words.

I tried to explain that I was afraid of them not accepting Alice, as had happened to my wishes many times before. I knew my father was sitting there listening to me, as my mother kept referring to his presence throughout.

Finally, my Father took the phone from my mother. His voice was curt.

"Leave that *wench* and come back to India. I will find you a suitable girl from our caste. We will forget any of this happened and move on."

Something broke in me when he said that.

"What the hell are you saying?" I yelled at him. "You are talking about my wife. Will you leave your wife and go if someone asks you to? You are a stupid egoistic man and you have been this way all your life. Everything I wanted in my life, you tried to control. I will not let you do anything more with my life choices ever again."

My words came pouring without restraint.

There was a long pause.

"You are right. You are you. You can do anything you want. You don't need this stupid egoistic man anymore. You are dead to me, Arjuna, as of this minute. I am going to perform the ritual for the dead for you, and mourn your loss."

I could hear my mother screaming in the background at my father.

"If your mother somehow decides to stay in touch with you after this, she too will be dead to me. Don't try to connect with me again and I will not try to connect with you."

That was the last time I spoke to my father or mother.

Alice was distraught about how she had caused a break in my relationship with my parents. She advised me many many times to call my parents and make amends. She bought me a ticket to India and some gifts for her in-laws so I could travel back home and make things right. But I think I too had inherited some of the egoistic stubbornness. I refused to call my parents or go to India.

What was liberating in the beginning, became a burden of guilt with time. Slowly, I began yearning for connection with my parents. I felt incomplete, ungrateful. I tried calling my mother's phone. There was no response. I tried many times after. But I was never successful."

I am crying as I narrate my past.

A lot more had to be said, but I shake myself out of my memory trip. The chai has gone cold. I drink it up quickly.

Krishna is sitting quietly, listening.

That is what I love about him. He never seems to judge, even with his eyes.

'What about you Krishna? How was your father like?'

Krishna has a strange look on his face as he considers my question.

It seems to me he is reaching into a trove of memories that he has heaped in a dusty forgotten corner.

"My father was passionate about sweets' he says finally. 'My father started his business selling Jalebis on the roadside and made it into the most successful sweet shop in town. He called it Rajashree Mithai, after my mother."

I am curious about the journeys of this gentle tea seller of
Kedarnath, who knew so much, spoke so little, and left only
the softest of footprints on the places he trod. I am happy
that Krishna is opening up about his life journeys now.

"My father had only two loves- his family and his sweet
shop. My brothers are...were older than me by 10 and 12
years. They started working in the sweet shop soon after
their schooling. My brothers were good with business. With
their help, my father expanded Rajashree sweets and built
more branches. My brothers were married and had kids.
We all lived together in this big home that my father had
built in the middle of town. People were coming from all
over to get Rajashree sweets. Money was pouring in.

I was the odd one out in the family- I did not have a mind
for business, and I was not street smart. Right from my
childhood poetry and philosophy held a bigger sway than
money. I don't know why. Perhaps I took after my mother.
Life was good. My brothers and my sisters-in-law were kind
to me.

And then my mother died. I was about 17 at that time.

After her passing, my father was a changed man.

He was lost, angry, bitter. My mother had taken care of his
every need from the moment he woke up to the minute
he went to sleep. She was his safe place, his shelter from
the vagaries of business. Without her, even his business
began to suffer. He started being unreasonable with people,
unkind to even those who had worked closely with him for
a long time. That behavior extended into our home as well.
Every day at home there were bitter fights and accusations.
Whenever my brothers brought up the idea of letting them
run the business, he would run into a massive rage and

accuse them of trying to steal his legacy. The way they were being treated made my sisters-in-law angry as well. Slowly, my father was breaking up the wonderful castle he had built, and he did not even know it. We lived in a divided mansion- my father with his illusion of control on one side, and my brothers and their wives on the other.

Sometimes the unkindest things are done with love.

I was the only person in the family that did not care about money. Which is why my father trusted me to talk about his suspicions about my brothers. No amount of convincing from my end changed his view that people were out to get his wealth. This singled-out trust began to irk my brothers and my sisters-in-law, and it began to show in the way they were treating me. My father's health began to deteriorate as well and he became bedridden. Even while my brothers ran the business, my father was still very much in control.

The final blow came two years after my mother's death. My father called us all to his room, and with a lawyer present, announced that all his wealth, including his shops and the home we lived in, would be inherited by me after him. I was shocked, and so was everyone present. It turned out, that my father had set up a mole within our home. This person, I never found out who it was, had let my father know that my sisters-in-law were discussing privately that they were eager for my father to die so they could move on. No amount of my pleading to change his mind helped.

My brothers walked out of the business and our home that very day. My brothers and my sisters-in-law surmised that I was the mole. After all, I was the one who spoke to my father the most, and I had succeeded in inheriting my father's wealth. My father's actions had driven an irreparable wedge between me and my brothers. They cut

off all communication from us. Only me and my ailing
father and a horde of servants were left in that huge cold
mansion. I was so angry with my father for his inability to
see what was important.

A few months after this happened, I had an accident.

A car veered out of nowhere into the bazaar where I was
shopping and crashed into me. I was left in a coma. When
I woke up in the hospital room, only one person was in
the room. It was Nana, an old lady who had served our
family for the longest time. She was in tears. I came to
know through her that many things had happened during
my time at the hospital. Turned out the accident was not
really an accident. One of my brothers had been arrested
for orchestrating it.

My father's condition had worsened and he was almost at
death's bed.

I was heart petrified. To think that my own brothers would
want to have me killed, for no fault of mine, destroyed me
inside.

My father died a few weeks after my return from the
hospital.

I was now the owner of Rajshree sweets and the mansion. I
was 19 years old. I could do what I wanted to do with these
assets. I walked right over to my father's lawyer. I asked that
he draft a new document that said that everything I now
owned belonged to my brothers. I had it sent to my two
brothers along with a letter apologizing for any pain my
father may have caused them.

I packed my clothes and took some loose cash and walked
away."

He pauses to smile.

"So you see Arjuna, when you shared your story with me, I could completely empathize. I know what it means to walk away. I know what it feels like to lose your legs and gain your wings in a moment.

With time, I wandered, learned to make tea, and ended up here in the mountains.

It has been so many decades now. But I have not gone back to Mathura. I sometimes wonder how Rajashree Sweets is doing, if it is still there. I wonder how my brothers and my sisters-in-law are doing, if they have other kids, and if they found happiness after receiving the wealth they so wanted. But then I remind myself that the past is only a story I tell myself. I can color it any which way I want. After all, the only purpose of all that has happened is to lead me to this moment. So very little is needed for a person who lives the drama of life one moment at a time, and carries no baggage of the past, isn't it?"

Chapter Seven

Reflections In the Cave: Inner Peace

"Is there a shortcut for inner peace?" I ask Krishna out of the blue.

Krishna ponders the question dutifully.

"I believe that inner peace is a moment-by-moment choice. It is not a destination or a trophy that you win and display on your mantle. It is a way of seeing and experiencing the world - you become the peace that you seek. It may take many journeys to get to the choice. But for the ones who have made that choice, no other possibility exists."

"Have you found your inner peace, Krishna?"

He laughs.

"Well, I think I have found my version of inner peace. To me, inner peace is being able to see my true place in the universe with no fear or attachment. I will tell you a story of a man who I think found his inner peace.

Naranath Branthan, the madman of Naranath, lay down by the burning pyres of the cremation grounds waiting for sleep to come. Goddess Kali, in all her fearsome glory, accompanied by the most fearsome ghouls, strolled through the cremation grounds. While every life form fled from her terrifying presence, Naranath was not moved. He sat and stared calmly at Kali and her demons. Kali was surprised and asked him to move to a different place. Naranath responded that he cannot go anywhere where she is not already, and she cannot go anywhere where he is already not. Kali, knowing she has no power over a man without fear, granted him a boon. This mad man with elephantiasis on his left leg, do you know what he did? He did not ask for healing or wealth. He instead asked that she can move his pain from his left leg to his right leg. So, a man like Naranath, who is in perfect harmony with himself, has no fear, no desire for validation. Everything he sees is perfect, even his elephantiasis."

"But how can we hope for inner peace when there is so much suffering? Everywhere I turn I see suffering. When I see people laugh I feel that they are ignorant of the truth or they are ignoring the truth of all-pervasive suffering.

Beyond the everyday illusions of what makes us laugh and smile, there is only the ragged, leprosied face of suffering. She is dreadful to look at. Yet, when you are compelled to turn away and run, resist. Stay a while and look at her. You will see that even suffering is a veil of illusion waiting to be lifted. As you sit with suffering and look into her bloodied eyes with love, and converse with her, you will see she is just joy with blotchy makeup.

Sometimes it takes deep conversations with suffering, to discover inner peace. Grief and happiness, two representations of the same deep spiritual experiences, become inseparable.

So learn to sit with your own suffering and listen. Soon you will learn to listen to the suffering of others too, and you will realize that we are all in this together. Since we will understand how suffering feels for us, we will not add to the suffering of others, perhaps even seek to relieve theirs. This is compassion. And it all starts with listening."

After our conversation, I sit and ponder at all the times I have run away from discomfort. If only I had been courageous enough to meet my discomforts head-on, my life would have taken a different path.

And Alice would still have been alive.

Chapter Eight

Alice

Remembering Alice, I gain wings, but burn my heart.

I try not to remember her because it hurts me so much.

But today the sun shines through the branches of deodar trees in flickering slivers of molten gold, like the golden tresses of my blue-eyed angel, and I cannot help thinking about Alice.

When I left for the US from India to pursue a two years master's degree in Computer sciences, the path ahead was already laid out. I would tread the well-worn path of the thousands and thousands of others like me who come to the US from India for higher education: find a job as soon as possible, get permanent residency, return to India, marry a girl of parents' choice, return to job, get American citizenship, have kids, navigate cross-cultural dilemmas as kids grow old, watch them pursue their paths, retire, die.

For one year I stick close to plan. I study hard, share a cramped apartment with four other students, work as a teaching assistant to support my meager living, learn to cook and clean- which I had never done back home in India, stick close to the Indian student community in New

Orleans, call home every week, and dream of a well-paying job.

At the end of the first year, one of my classmates, an American student invites me to an end-of-year party in his home. It is a simple party in his backyard- lots of barbeque and beer- neither of which I can consume. There is active conversation about football and politics which I cannot relate to. I find a chair in the corner of the backyard sipping lemonade and munching on chips, waiting for an opportunity to leave without appearing rude.

Just when I am ready to excuse myself and go home, my classmate, the one who invited me to the party, walks over to me. With him is a girl about my age, perhaps younger. I look at her and immediately remember a Christmas greeting card from my childhood. On that greeting card was the painting of an angel- rosy cheeks, golden hair, blue eyes, a gentle smile that radiated kindness. I cannot help thinking that this girl must have modeled for that painting.

"Arjuna, hey buddy, I want to introduce you to Alice, my cousin. Alice this is Arjuna, my buddy from India."

Alice and I shake hands.

"So Arjuna," my classmate continues, "Alice is trying to become vegetarian. I have no idea why anyone would want to do that." He grins. "I told her there is one other person in the world who does not eat meat. So I thought I could get you two sharing notes. You guys chat. I must go grab a beer."

He walks away.

All my life, I have been painfully shy around people. I do not expect my conversation with this beauty to last long. But Alice and I talk and talk. She laughs easily, listens patiently, does not judge me when I bumble. I am captivated.

I do not want the evening to end.

I learn that Alice is an undergrad student at my university, majoring in English, that she aspires to become a teacher, loves kids and puppies, hopes to teach in elementary school. I learn that she is from Baton Rouge, an hour away from New Orleans, and that her parents and two brothers still live there. She opens up to me easily - this brown-skinned stranger from the other side of the planet.

We decide to meet again the next weekend.

The second year of my master's program turns out to be the most beautiful time of my life. It soon becomes obvious to us that what we have between us is more than friendship. We spend every minute we can together. Others begin noticing it too. Whenever Alice visits me in my apartment, my roommates find excuses to leave so we can have the space to ourselves. She and I would both be finishing college that year- I with a master's and she with an undergraduate degree. It is not long before we start dreaming of a future together.

As my reality with Alice blossoms, I am also painfully aware that I am reluctant to talk about us to my parents. Alice cannot understand why an independent adult would find the necessity to be bound so much by his parents' expectations. She asks me, again and again, to talk to my parents and lay it out in the open. I know I should listen to her, but every time that thought comes up, I think of my father's disapproval and my mother's disappointment. I tell Alice that I will talk about us at an appropriate time. Once, I try introducing Alice to my parents as a friend. My father makes a veiled comment that discourages me from trying again.

In reality, I am just a coward. And this cowardice will come to hurt me for the rest of my life.

Alice takes me to meet her family for Thanksgiving that year. Hers is a middle-class family- her father is an insurance salesman and her mother is a nurse. They have lived in Baton Rouge all their lives. I can see that neither her parents nor her brothers are impressed by Alice's choice. But they welcome me into their home nonetheless. Alice is the youngest in their home and her happiness matters to them. They ask me about my family and if there is a possibility of connecting with them. I defer that to a different day.

When college ends, I find a job in a small software startup in New Orleans. Alice starts a one-year program for her teacher certification and finds a job as a teacher's aide to support herself. We find a small apartment in Uptown New Orleans, a few blocks from the street car, and move in together. Life is beautiful for us. I continue to speak to my parents every week, but I decide not to visit India. Alice has given up trying to convince me to let my parents in on our relationship. That would have been the easiest and most meaningful thing to do. But I am lost in my dark imaginings.

A year after we move in together, Alice and I start discussing marriage. She wants me to take her to India and introduce

her to the world I grew up in before our wedding. I promise
her that I would someday, but not yet.

That day never happens.

Alice is getting restless about my waiting for the right
moment. We quarrel every time this topic comes up. Then
we reconcile. There comes a point she does not care that
I am not talking about us to my parents. I promise her
that my issue with my parents will not come between us.
She believes me. On a warm summer day in July, we get
married. Her family, my friends, and us. It is a beautiful
occasion. Everything is perfect. Except that my parents are
not there to bless us.

Memory trains travel on bumpy tracks. I cannot remember
my happy time with Alice without thinking about the most
painful turn in my road- the day I killed her and the events
that lead up to it.

Our initial days after our wedding were absolute heaven. I
was surprised how much two humans can be so much in
love with each other. But then the call from my parents
came when they found out that I had married without their
knowledge or consent. The cracks started appearing.

After my break-up phone call with my father, my ego did
not allow me to call him again. I was angry with my mother
though for not supporting me, but I wanted to talk to her
even if it was to tell her how angry I was with her. But I
did not. Alice was of course upset and angry that my father
had called her a wench. But she was the first to let go of

the anger. She urged me to make peace with my parents not long after the incident. I went back to my old tactic of saying that I would address it at the right moment.

A year goes by. I am thriving in my job. Alice has passed her teaching certification requirements. We are very much in love. I have not tried calling India. They have not tried calling me. I try not to think about that lingering lesion.

I am content with Alice and the time I spend with her. I have not stayed in touch with friends from my past. One of my roommates from the University calls me on a Friday night. He conveys his condolences for my mother's loss. It is a moment of sheer horror. I come to learn that he had visited India recently and through his parent's friends come to know that my mother had passed six months ago. Cardiac failure. I think there is a misunderstanding. I disconnect and call my parents' number immediately.

"What happened to Amma!?" I scream when my father picks up the phone.

"Who is this?" my father asks sarcastically.

"What happened to Amma?" I yell. "Someone here told me that she had a cardiac arrest."

"My wife Mrs. Saroja Venkatraman died a few months ago of a cardiac arrest. Since she does not have any living children I did the final rites for her."

My head is pounding.

I explode.

"Why didn't you....You egoistic bastard. I..."

The line disconnects.

I call again. And again. And again.

My father picks up the phone.

"Listen, sir," he tells me curtly as he picks up the phone, "please do not call this number and bother me. And do not try to visit. You are not welcome here."

He hangs up again. I keep calling to no avail.

When I call again the next morning, I learn that the phone line is permanently disconnected.

They say time heals everything. For me, time only hid my pain under layers and layers of everyday realities. Whenever the memories of my mother came calling, I would shove them back into a dark room and pretend that everything was great. Along the way, I started drinking- first on the weekends to numb my guilt, but then ever so often, no excuses needed. This created a rift between me and Alice. We were both doing well in our jobs. She had found a job teaching in an elementary school which she loved. We still loved each other. But we were quarreling more and more. The alcohol was becoming my excuse to say unkind things to her. I would inevitably apologize and we would patch up. But patches are patches - they are held together by threads that fray. Alice began going away to her parent's in Baton Rouge during the weekends to escape my toxicity. My relationship with her parents which was never really cozy at any point began even more jagged.

Another five slow years dragged by.

Around the sixth anniversary of our wedding, after
a particularly emotional weekend of quarreling and
reconciliation, I decided to sober up. I threw away the
bottles, made promises to leave behind my past, and signed
up for Alcoholics Anonymous meetings.

Life seemed to be finally getting back on track.

Finally, the happy news came.

Alice was pregnant.

The anticipation of the new baby was a healing force
between me and Alice's parents. I had long given up trying
to contact my own father.

It is the Thanksgiving day of 2007.

Alice is seven months pregnant. It has been our tradition
to spend thanksgiving with Alice's parents, spend the night
with them, and return the following day for black Friday
shopping. This year there is a lot of shopping to be done.
We are excited

Everything is going well. It is pretty late in the night. The
conversation turns to baby names. Alice's dad asks me what
we are planning to call our baby. I tell him that the baby
will be named after my grandparents as has always been
a tradition in our family. He thinks it is a bad idea. He
knows that I have no more ties to my lineage. For some
reason, this irks me, much more than it should. I get into

an argument with him about it. He does not back off. My brothers-in-law join in. Unkind words are exchanged. The women try to pacify. No one is listening. A beautiful Thanksgiving evening unravels into chaos.

I do not want to stay the night. I tell Alice that I am heading back home to New Orleans and she can stay here if she wants. She is angry, but she joins me. She insists she drives though. I agree.

We are both silently fuming as we drive back on the empty roads that Thanksgiving night. We should have remained silent.

But she breaks the silence.

"You are a jerk!" she tells me.

"How dare you," I yell back. "Your father was the one who disrespected me"

"No. All he said was there is no point in holding to your tradition when you are no longer linked to it."

"And who said I am no longer linked to it? You know I was on a happy track until I met you. I would have married a girl they chose for me, someone from my own community. There would have been no confusion. But I married you. And because of you, I lost my parents and my peace of mind."

"So now you blame me?" she is crying. But she is also speeding. "You have no idea how many sacrifices I have made and continue to make for you. You are a childish, stubborn man. Just like your dad. And know what? You are a coward! That is the honest simple truth. If you were man enough you would have faced your parents head-on and stood up for your decision to marry me. But you were scared. You made excuses. Look what that led to. And now, you want to turn all that on me!"

I am burning up with anger.

"You are right," I yell, "all this was a mistake. I want out."

And then the single moment that would change the course of my life.

I reach out to the steering wheel that Alice is holding and jerk it toward me. I am not sure what I am thinking. I perhaps hope that this would bring the car to a stop.

Alice loses control.

She screams as the car veers off the highway into an access road. Her foot is still on the accelerator. It all happens in a few seconds.

The car rams against the wall separating the highway and the sideroad.

The last thing I hear is a loud sickening crash of crumpling metal and the screaming of my wife.

The lingering sounds of that crash are muffled by the pervasive blanket of this mountain's silence.

I share this chapter with Alice to Krishna on a cold winter evening.

As always, he listens carefully and patiently without judgment.

"The sad part is, Krishna," I say with a wry smile, "Alice was absolutely right. I was a coward. Even after her death, I did not come clean about the incidents that led to the crash. I never told anyone that I had pulled on the steering wheel. All they surmised was that we had had an argument and Alice had become so distraught that she lost control of her driving and crashed. Her parents spent a lot of time trying to get me to share the details. I was afraid."

I pause to gather myself.

"In fact, I let all this fester for another year. Alice's family stopped talking to me. I still went to work. Made money. But day by day, it became more and more difficult for me to look at myself in the mirror. Every time I saw any of the things that belonged to Alice, her final words came back to taunt me. I tried going to churches and temples. But none of the Gods wanted to visit a place so dark and sad as my mind. I made appointments with doctors. But I never kept my appointments. My trip to India was my final push to tie at least one loose end with my father. And here I am."

I laugh. A sad dry and cynical laugh.

Krishna knows that I am not seeking advice at this moment. He knows that I am reliving a dark memory with him in confidence.

There is some more silence in the cave.

He lies down on his bedding, facing the roof of the cave, and adjusts his blanket.

"Everybody is entitled to improbable gifts of grace, Arjuna," he whispers. "Everyone"

Chapter Nine

Reflections In the Cave: Love and Attachment

Something about Krishna's reflections on love and attachment on the tape I am listening to today has me wondering.

'All universe is energy. It throbs with truths and plans that only it knows

I am but a tiny speck within this pulsating orb

When I vibrate in rhythm with the universe, I discover harmony

When I vibrate out of rhythm, I find dissonance

Attachment stops me from vibrating with the universe

The more I am free of attachment, the more easily I vibrate.

Attachment comes to me in many ways

It comes to be in the form of love- for my family, for my body

It comes to me in the form of fear- of loss, of freedom

It comes to me in the form of desire- for wealth, for fame

It comes to me in the form of illusions- of permanence, of self-importance

As long as strings exist, I do not fully vibrate with the universe.'

I seek out Krishna for explanations.

Krishna tells me that attachment is the spring of all suffering. He tells me that a person who is not attached to his ego or possessions or emotions cannot experience suffering. But no one, not even the most illustrious of us, are free from attachment, he points out. He narrates the story of Jada Bharata, after whom Bharat, now called India, got its name.

"The Hindu way of life," says Krishna, "dictates that a man pass his time on earth in four phases- as a student, as a family man, as a spiritual seeker, and finally as a renunciate seeking liberation from the cycles of life and death. King Bharata, the greatest among kings, after excelling in his first two roles, retires to the forest to seek spiritual knowledge and freedom. He sits and meditates in his humble abode when fate places a baby fawn in his care. The king saves the fawn, nurtures it, and inevitably becomes attached to it as a father would to a beloved child. His waking hours are filled with concern for the safety of the little deer, so much so that he loses interest in his spiritual quest. When many years later death comes calling, he dies thinking of his deer rather than the ideals of liberation and paradise which would have freed him from the eternal cycles of suffering. The man whose powerful mind was able to break past his lifelong attachments to power, comforts, and family, could not break free of his attachment to that little deer. And therefore he continues his cycle of birth and rebirth- when he could have easily stepped out of it."

"Which is why Arjuna," he continues, "there is love that liberates and love that binds. If you love hoping to be loved back, you suffer. Because the nature of the universe is to love unconditionally. By adding expectations to your love you go against the grain of the universe. So we must love, as the universe does, because we can and because we must. Always taking care not become bound to the outcome of love- since therein lies sorrow. The reward of love is the act of loving itself. For when we love deeply, without expectations, without fear, we manifest God and God becomes us."

I wish someone had taught me this truth at the outset. My experience of love would have been so different.

Chapter Ten

Sita

King Dandaka, filled with lust and arrogance, brutally rapes and defiles Arajaa. To the king, anything that lives on his land is his possession. Arajaa is only a child when she is raped. Dandaka destroys the innocence of this young girl, and leaves her bleeding in the forest, laughing, his lust satiated. Arajaa's father is a sage. Seeing what has happened to his daughter, the sage curses the king and his land. In seven days, the story is said, the king and all his land burned and perished in the fury of a father's wrath.

Arajaa means without impurity.

There are many Arajaas in our land. There are even more Dandakas.

But not all Arajaas have fathers that avenge evil men.

Sometimes the Dandakas win.

Some mendicants prefer cities, some prefer suburbs.

I prefer the suburbs.

Begging is a profession that generates revenue. And it includes all sorts of players.

I have encountered affluent men and women who see begging as their day job, and not as the desperation of survival. They arrive in autos and taxis, change into begging costumes, beg for a designated time and head home with their loot. They pay protection money to strong men and sometimes the police, and in return, their territories are protected. With experience, they have honed the art of appearance and ask that generate the most revenue. They see no qualms in soliciting from the middle-class man who is likely poorer than they are. Entire ecosystems have been created around the revenue that begging generates- including that very dark space of exploitation of children and the physically and mentally maimed.

But not all beggars are charlatans, and poverty in India is very real. Desperation is real. Human hopelessness is real. Mental illnesses that lead to destitution are very real.

But I see less of this in the suburbs, simply because the revenue stream is thinner and less predictable. A suburb is not the place for the ambitious beggar.

I am not an ambitious beggar.

For about three months now I have camped in a scrapyard on the edge of a small town. The last houses of this part of town taper off into a smattering of lazily constructed houses on a dirt lane. The scrapyard is across from the last house of this town- a small pale green and yellow tiled structure that has been built without love. The scrapyard has a lot of used tires and disused car parts, and jagged edges of metal screaming of tetanus. I have managed to clear a spot between a pile of tires and stretch a plastic tarp over the tire canopy. I usually sleep out in the open, so this is an upgrade. I can see myself staying here for a while. I have also found a hot spot not far from where I am camped- a little bazaar street with a church and a mosque with significant foot traffic. I have built a routine. Wake up, stare at the street, wander to the bazaar around lunch, eat, wander back to the scrapyard for a nap, wander back to the bazaar if I felt like it, or simply sit and watch children play in the open space between the scrapyard and the street, sleep and repeat. Time moves slowly here. But I am in no rush.

She is about 9 years old. She lives in the last house on the street overlooking the scrapyard. I believe she goes to school during the day. Most evenings, usually after dark, she comes and sits on a stone block outside the scrapyard and plays by herself. She draws little squares on the sand and plays hopscotch. Sometimes she stays there late into the evening. Then her mother comes out of the house and calls, and she goes home. I have only seen her mother in the semi-dark, in the light of the lamp outside the house. She seems like a woman in her thirties. I see a lot of men come and go in the evenings. It is easy for me to surmise what her profession is.

It is a warm humid evening.

I do not feel like walking down to the bazaar today.

I have in my hand a piece of chalk on the road that I found walking home this afternoon.

I am drawing something on the ground. I notice the little girl peering at me, her hands resting on the tiny wall separating the scrapyard from the road. Her head is tilted in rapt attention.

After a while, she comes over.

"She has a fat nose," she comments about the picture of the girl I have drawn on the ground. "I like her."

She smiles. The kind, happy smile of innocence.

"Draw a dog."

I try to draw a dog. With a big nose.

She laughs.

"Dogs don't look like that!"

I give her the chalk.

"You draw."

I feel strange talking to a child. I feel like an equal. I realize I have not had a conversation like this in a very long time.

She grabs the chalk from me and starts drawing her dog. Her head is twisted in rapt attention. She erases parts of her chalk drawing with her hands and continues. In the end, there is a cryptic shape of an animal behind a mess of chalk powder.

"I like your dog." I smile. She smiles too.

"I have color pieces of chalk at home," she says proudly. "I will get them tomorrow. Then we can draw a color dog."

"Ok"

She hears her mother call.

Her smile fades for a second.

"I will come tomorrow," she whispers conspiratorially. And runs toward her house. I see her mother talking to her in the distance. She is pointing toward the scrapyard. Her mother looks in my direction. I can see them talk some more and go inside.

The next day, the little girl is back again. With colored chalks as she promised.

We draw more dogs, cats, and people.

She likes to talk. About everything.

"Did your mom say it is okay for you to come and play here?"

"Yes," she replies. "I told her the madman is not dangerous and that he likes to draw."

It takes a while for me to register that the madman she is talking about is me.

I laugh. I try to think how I appear to a nine-year-old- with matted dreadlocks, an unkempt beard, and torn clothes.

"Are you dangerous?" she asks, with a little lilt of her head. She is looking at me intently. She wants to be sure. Then she seems to make up her mind.

"No, you are not dangerous," she declares.

Then she starts drawing on the ground again. There is silence. I am not sure what to say.

"You are not like some of the men who come to meet amma"

It takes a while for this to sink in.

"What happened?"

She does not answer. I see her little face sag. I begin to understand.

"Are those men trying to hurt you? You must tell your mother if anyone tries to hurt you."

"It's ok," she whispers. "I have this."

She looks around and takes out something from the inner folds of her skirt. She opens her palms to reveal a tiny pocket knife. It is the kind of folding knife you get for a couple of rupees in village fairs. You cannot even cut a raw mango with this knife. But in her little mind, this is her safety net.

"Listen," I tell her firmly, "I know you are a strong girl. But if someone is bad to you you should tell your mother."

She does not answer.

"Please?" I entreat.

"Ok"

After she leaves, I realize I do not know her name.

She comes again the next day. She has some sugar jujubes in her palms - chewy candies that you buy for cheap in roadside shops. I used to love them when I was young. She shares a few with me.

I am grateful for this little child.

"Did you talk to your mother?"

"I will"

"You promised"

"I will"

She eats her share of jujubes silently.

"My name is Sita. What is yours?"

I laugh.

"I am the madman. Don't you know?"

"Do you have any other name?"

"Not anymore."

"Ok"

She accepts my answer.

I tear up at her innocence. For a while, the world seems more hopeful.

She stays there for a while- talking and drawing.

Then she runs away.

Sita comes every day. Her arrival has become part of my daily routine. I look forward to the evenings so I can meet the little girl.

I learn that she has a fair idea of her mother's work. After all, she is in a corner of the room when her mother's clients come in the night, expected to be asleep. I feel enraged and helpless.

Hers is a lonely childhood. It is difficult for a prostitute's daughter to keep friends. The men who come to their house at night with gifts disown them in daylight.

No one else speaks with Sita or her mother.

I think Sita feels safe with the madman.

Her scream pierces the darkness.

I wake up with a start. It is dark except for the dim street lamp.

Sita is running toward my scrapyard.

A half-naked man is running behind her.

In the distance, I see Sita's mother stagger out of her door and crash to the ground.

Sita continues to run toward me. Her clothes are ripped apart.

Perhaps others hear her scream, but do not want to intervene. Perhaps they are quietly telling themselves that the prostitute and her child are getting their comeuppance.

I rush toward her, stepping over rusty metal and shreds of tires. Sita rushes into my arms. I stand between her and the man. The man in front of me is built like a gorilla. He is snarling, almost frothing at his mouth. His eyes are screaming lust. He will not be stopped by a mad beggar.

He lunges toward me, and the little girl cowers behind.

I eye an old exhaust pipe on a pile of tires.

In an instant I grab it and bash the man on the head with all my might. He screams as he falls.

Years of my pent-up rage boil out into the open. I am angry at myself. I am angry at the world. I am angry at existence. I am angry at the Gods who see injustice but hide behind stupid stories of karma.

I do not hold back. I hit, I slash, I thrust with fury. The exhaust pipe crushes his skull and gouges his eyes. I do not stop, even to the screaming pleas of Sita. It takes a few minutes before someone physically tries to stop me. Someone in the street has decided to intervene. They did not intervene for the little girl a few minutes ago.

I throw the exhaust pipe at the crowd that is beginning to gather around the scene. The noisy, despicable vultures are closing in. Sita is still cowering behind me. She slips me her little knife. Perhaps she hopes it will protect me. I turn back, and for a second see the tear-stained face of the little child.

I shrug her off and begin to run.

People yell at me to stop.

No one seems to want to follow. Perhaps they do not mean to hurt me.

I do not want to wait to find out.

I run into the darkness with every ounce of my strength.

I am crying.

I have left behind my little friend amidst a pack of wolves.

Chapter Eleven

Reflections in the Cave: Journeys

The snow covers up everything on winter days.

It is tempting to paint on this shimmering white canvas with smatterings of memories from my travels.

Memories...

I am lying in the frugal shade of a stone stupa on a burning summer afternoon. Another stray, a dog, has chosen to share this receding spot of shadow with me. We do not compete with each other for the comfort of shadow. We know that after a while, even this sliver of refuge will disappear. For now, we sleep to escape. But I am tired of sleeping.

I have a scab on my leg. I know better than picking at it. No good ever comes from picking scabs. But I do pick my scab. It is an infinitely grotesque and useless task- I will suffer for many days onward- but it keeps me busy. Teasing the dried-out piece of flesh seems to give me purpose in the moment- relief from the ever-increasing itch if only for a brief instant. I know I will hurt for the next few days while I wait for healing from this moment of perverse pleasure. A new scab will form and there will be another lazy afternoon when I will pick at them. Until someday my attention turns to something else, or it simply becomes too painful to pick.

Picking physical scabs has so much less fallout than picking mental scabs.

But the latter we seem to do all the time.

After all, they are hidden behind the masks we wear.

I sit outside the iron gates of a restaurant's patio, hidden behind the shadow of a tree.

The smell of delicious food wafts across. It appeals to me in a way, only the very hungry can understand

If I stay quiet, no one will notice and come out to drive me away. This is a routine I have come to know too well. Stay hidden and the scraps will come.

Restaurants do not want beggars loitering around their customers. The sight of us poor folk could make their customers feel uncomfortable, and lose appetite. The reality of suffering jars their private bubble. In this bubble, they have learned to feel safe in their pursuits, their comparisons, and little stories they have made up about reality.

They need not be reminded that what separates them from the other realities is a small fence. To learn to become oblivious to suffering is perhaps the only way to afford celebrations.

On the restaurant patio, three middle-aged women are dining at the table closest to the fence.

From their conversations I surmise one of them is a visitor from the USA, celebrating her vacation with her old friends. They are retelling stories, creating memories oblivious to the world around them. She could have been me. My mind scans their conversation for hints that will help me label them in ways that will make them feel small to me. Feeling like a victim gives me a sense of power. This is my bubble.

I will need it for warmth when the restaurant closes and the cold silent night descends upon me with its haunting echoes of '*it could have been*'.

For many weeks now I have been sleeping in an abandoned culvert pipe near a temple. It is a strategic position. I do not have to stray too far to beg, and the culvert pipes are large enough to give me a comfortable retreat from the elements. Sometimes dogs walk in and share the space with me. We tolerate each other.

A young man, in his mid-twenties, notices me in the pipe. He drives a small delivery van. He stops the vehicle near my pipe and comes over to talk to me. He wants to know if I am hungry and if I need a place to stay. I do not want to be taken away to an asylum again. I am hungry, but I tell him

I am not. Still, he goes to the van and comes with a packet of food- simple south Indian food, fresh and hot. He sits next to me, opens the food packet, and passes it to me. The aroma reminds me of my mother's cooking.

I hesitate. But hunger takes over.

I gobble up the food.

He offers me a bottle of water before he leaves.

The next day he comes back again. I am surprised that he is not repulsed by my sores or stench. He talks to me as an equal.

He asks me for my story- where I am from, what home is for me, if I know someone who can take me back.

I do not reply.

After I eat, he asks if I want a place to stay.

I tell him I am happy here.

He comes every day. I have started to look forward to the minutes I spend with this young man. He likes to talk while I eat. I come to learn that he was an aspiring chef who gave up his dreams to feed the mentally ill. One day he brings a barber's kit. He tells me that he is going to give me a haircut and a shave. I protest, but he wins me over with his gentle insistence. For the first time in many months, I look like a human being. For a brief while, I feel like one.

What fear and regret could not achieve, human kindness seems to accomplish.

Yet, the next morning, I walk away from the culvert pipe.

Perhaps I am afraid of hope itself.

Chapter Twelve

Karna

In the Mahabaratha, fate destines Karna, a demigod, to be brought up in a family of untouchables. Immensely talented but despised because of his low status, Karna is shamed in a large gathering and denied opportunities. King Duryodhana, the chief antagonist of the Mahabaratha, defends Karna in his moment of shame and makes him a king. Karna never forgets the generosity of Duryodhana. He sticks to Duryodhana through his many misadventures, knowing that it will cause his destruction, and ultimately does give up his life for his benefactor.

There are Karnas around us- but they are rare and few.

It is now three days since I attacked Sita's assailant. I have walked and walked, as much as my strength would carry me, trying to create physical distance between myself and the murder. I have no destination. India is a land of many jurisdictions. I hope a non-entity like me will be able to melt into the throng of a far away part of India and escape retribution.

It is late in the evening. I sit by an eatery outside a small town, exhausted from a day of walking. The air is heady with the smell of frying eggs, parottas, curry leaves, and masalas; the incessant clanging of metal spoons against the woks is making me salivate. I sit in the half shadows, dreaming of food and hoping that some kind patron of that eatery will notice me.

There is a pot of water and a plastic mug on a table near where I am sitting. This is the shop's wash basin substitute. A burly man with greasy hair comes out of the tiffin center to wash his hands. I look at him, he notices me looking at him. Something about me seems to raise his ire.

"Hey ..... what are you looking at?"

He is speaking in Telugu, a language I understand somewhat but cannot speak well.

I nod my head and look away.

"I am talking to you ..... Don't you dare look away. Waiting to see who you can thieve from, arent you?"

He is yelling, attracting attention.

That is the last thing I want now.

I shake my head to indicate I am not a thief and fold my palms to indicate submission.

This does not appease the self-appointed vigilante.

"So you are pretending to be dumb? I know buggers like you. You sit and watch, follow people home, slit their throats and run with the money. Not in my town!"

He wants to create a scene. He is probably a little inebriated.

I slink further away from the glare of the tiffin center's tube lights.

A few people have gathered around to watch.

"Just a plain old beggar. Let him be." someone mutters half-heartedly.

The greasy-haired man is not satiated.

He advances toward me. I brace for his attack. I cannot afford to fight back.

A man walks out from the tiffin center. He is dressed in saffron robes and has vermillion and sacred ash smeared on his forehead. He is a Sadhu- a renunciate.

He gently places his hands on the shoulders of the aggressor.

"Let him go bhai," he says gently, "he means no harm."

The greasy man whirls around ready to yell, but he sees the sadhu.

This aggressor may confront many strongmen, but he will not dare oppose a holy man.

He steps back.

"I am only trying to protect our community, Swamiji" he says.

"I understand, bhai. But he is not a thief. I can see it. He is just a hungry lost soul." He turns toward me. "Come, bhaiyya. Have you eaten yet?"

He smiles at me.

Suddenly I feel safe. In the middle of all the chaos, I smile in relief.

That is how I met Karna.

After a hearty meal of parottas, we sit outside the tiffin center and talk.

Karna is a rare soul. He seems genuinely concerned for me, a stranger in his town who cannot speak the local language. He sits and listens, his eyes glisten with earnest curiosity. The more I talk with him, the more I feel I can trust him. I haven't felt trust in a long time now. It feels strange- this urge to trust someone and share my story.

I learn that Karna 'belongs' to a local Ashram. The spiritual leader of the Ashram is Prem Baba. Prem is love in Hindi. Karna tells me that love is the message of his chosen spiritual master. Karna had wandered the streets of this town without purpose, until a few years ago, when Prem Baba had rescued him and set him on a path of spiritual salvation. Since then, Karna had been on the streets, rescuing wayward souls and leading them to Prem Baba, who would guide them toward salvation.

The more I speak to Karna, the more I realize I have found my destination.

I ask Karna if he can take me to Prem Baba.

Karna is elated.

He does not know my past. He does not care to ask. All he sees is a suffering soul. And he wants to help.

'In love there is healing, and love knows no discrimination' he says.

Exactly the words I need to hear.

I go to Prem Baba's ashram with Karna.

Chapter Thirteen

God men

When I decided to come to Prem Baba's ashram with Karna, I expected to see a humble building with an intimate group of people. I realized walking in that the ashram was far from humble. The ashram is set on a very large tract of land in a suburban town. The massive central buildings that include the main hall, a temple, and the living quarters of Baba dwarf the man small buildings which serve as residences for the ashrams many devotees.

Karna, I discover, is loyal to Prem Baba, his spiritual master.

"My Baba saved my life, taught me the way of love," he says often. "Without Baba, I would have died drunk. I owe my life to him."

A few years ago, Karna had wandered into the ashram after seeing his drinking buddy die of liver cirrhosis. Baba's words had healed Karna, and Karna had never left.

Karna takes me to meet Prem Baba two days after I arrive at his Ashram. This happens on a Friday morning, soon after the weekly public discourses that Baba gives.

Prem Baba is a man in his late fifties. Long oiled back gray hair, neatly trimmed mustache, and beard, gold-rimmed glasses, prayer beads on his neck, his forehead white with sacred ash and vermillion. Baba sits on a golden throne in the big hall of the Ashram, flanked by his two trusty lieutenants, and devotees singing songs.

Twenty years ago, Prem Baba had experienced a divine revelation on a trip to the Himalayas. He had left behind his life as a government employee and become a spiritual seeker. The story of his spiritual awakening, his quotes, and pictures with celebrities are all over the walls of the ashram walls. Prem Baba is a celebrity. Politicians and police officials stream in and out of the Ashram to get his blessings and discuss local affairs.

Although Karna is one of the most loved people in the Ashram, he does not rank high in the power hierarchy of this place. It is because Karna does not care enough for these things. So we wait, till all the people are gone after darshan (visiting) with the Baba - the rich and the powerful getting first dibs.

Prem Baba greets Karna with a blessing.

"How are you, Karna?"

Karna bows in obeisance.

"By your grace, Babaji," he replies respectfully.

He turns toward me. I follow his cue and bow to Prem Baba.

"This is my new friend, Arjuna. He came to our Ashram two days ago. I have invited him to stay here with us and help around the place."

"Of course, Karna," Prem Baba smiles benevolently. "All seekers are welcome here."

He turns to me.

"Where do you come from Arjuna?'

"I was born in Chennai, Swamiji. Now, I am a vagabond. I have no place I call home."

"Everyone has a home in God, don't they? You can stay here as long as you want. The Ashram is always in need of good sevaks (volunteers)."

He strokes his beard.

"Karna and Arjuna were on the opposite teams in Mahabaratha. Here in Prem Baba's Ashram, even enemies become allies. That is the power of love."

He beams in the pride of his observation. Karna is thrilled. He falls at his master's feet and motions me to do the same. I comply.

There is something about PremBaba- his arrogant display of power and wealth, his incessant seeking of adulation, his differential treatment of the rich and the poor, his uncontrolled ambition for connections and power, his willingness to recycle the wisdom of others as his own- that puts me off. I am surprised that Karna is unable to see it. Karna adores Prem Baba and I do not want to challenge him. It is because, in my life on the streets, I have had the opportunity to witness others like him. Since I wanted nothing from these 'god-men', I could see them for who they were. Perhaps, if I had gone seeking godmen in my moments of hopelessness, I might have interpreted their words and actions to fulfill my void, and experienced miracles when there were none.

Godmen and godwomen, they seem to be marketed everywhere- on televisions, on billboards, on posters on roadsides. There is very little barrier to entry for this profession. All it takes is relentless cunning and moral turpitude to become a God-person. The sad part is that no religion or God has anything to do with their self-professed roles.

Sitting here in the cave with Krishna, I think about these unholy godpeople and their willing victims.

Krishna shares that he is saddened by the devastation of hope created by this rapacious lot.

"A true spiritual teacher realizes, as their very first awakening, that like every other being on this planet, they are conduits of eternal wisdom. They become humble because they have been afforded this realization. So they do not walk around with banners, seeking power and adulation.

The paradox of spiritual seeking is that once you really achieve what you have sought, the journey of getting there has made you realize that what you have sought is meaningless, So you really have to cross a certain mental boundary to achieve your seeking, but the process of crossing the boundary has elevated you such a place that your achievement now seems meaningless.

A person who has transgressed his boundaries of self becomes a reminder to all those who seek that there within them too lies the same boundless being. So the inspirer listens to the voice that has no words, but whose meanings are endless.

And their desire to be adulated puzzles me. When I look at you with adulation, you become unreachable. When I look at you with hate, you become untouchable. When I look at you with love, you become me. And then the walls come crumbling down. How can anyone who does not realize this simple truth hope to lead others spiritually?"

I spend a while contemplating his words.

"Perhaps people do not know how to seek out good spiritual masters?" I venture.

"I have long given up the notion that anyone needs a master," replies Krishna. "God wants us to each be unique and free. We do not need to be bound by anyone else's wisdom or truth, however intelligent that may be. To abandon our gift of freedom of spirit for people or their ideologies is to spit on the face of God.

Teachers come to us in many forms. Some teachers give us answers, some inspire us to ask the right questions. Some teachers simply remind us that we already have all the answers we need. If we are open, everyone and every experience can become our teachers. But no teacher should demand to be masters of anyone except their own selves, for to do so is unenlightened and selfish. A true teacher knows that his role is to be a bridge between our now and our seeking. We do not carry bridges with us after we cross them, do we? If the bridge insists that we must stay on it because it helped us cross, or asks to be carried with us as we journey along, is it really serving its purpose?"

He speaks the truth.

Krishna, my teacher, taught from a place of unassuming compassion. As much wisdom there was in his words, he taught me through his actions. My teacher taught me to look inside myself - even the dark, shame-filled corners of my mind- with love. He taught me to forgive myself and not be inwardly divided. He brought me back from the brink, yet took no credit for it.

I would have called him master. But Krishna would not have agreed to it. So I call him the gift that the universe chose to give me.

Chapter Fourteen

Reflections in the Cave: Religion

For whatever reason, I am remembering Prem Baba and I am comparing him to Krishna.

Devotees flock from all over the world to worship the God of the fields. Every aspect of life in Kedarnath has a pervading essence of religion woven into it.

Krishna is truly a man of Kedarnath.

Yet, I have not seen any display of religion from him. He does not quote religious texts as I have seen - there is no sacred ash or vermillion, no statues of gods in the cave, no sacred beads around his neck.

On this snowy evening in January, sitting next to the fire, supping on the gruel we had made in the afternoon, I ask him about this.

He laughs.

"Why would I search for a God elsewhere Arjuna, when he is already here?" He points to me, then touches his head.

He sees my confused look.

"When I was younger, I believed that Gods lived in statues and in holy places. I gave them many names, attributed them powers, and parroted stories of their origins. But along the way, I saw that what to me was a sacred idol with supernatural powers, was simply a piece of rock to someone else. It was true the other way around too. The only truth here was that the true nature and purpose of the rock was being a rock. The rock itself seemed perfectly content being a rock. All powers for this piece of nature had came from within me, from within my mind."

"Are you saying that religion is wrong?"

"Not at all. I am saying what your mind believes in is your truth. It is a truth that cannot be denied. But religion should not become your destination. I see that religion can be a step toward spiritual awakening, which is the unconscious seeking of the spirit to ask and understand this question: *who am I?* By understanding itself, the spirit seeks to reunite with a much larger universal consciousness."

Krishna can see I am struggling.

He smiles at me patiently.

"To try and imprison the vastness of consciousness, the energy that pervades all of life and the farthest corners of the universe, to a limitation of human imagination in the form of religion and stories is the greatest of tragedies. The infinite energy of consciousness does not change, in the same way that other physical forces do not. But human imagination changes depending on the context in which it is placed. The stories of religion arise from fear and often a perverted human desire for control. That is why religions emphasize sin and salvation, of human misery and miracles that change them. But to know the consciousness is to know freedom. To know that there is nothing more divine and blissful than vibrating in the all-engulfing energy of the universe- because then we control nothing, own nothing, fear nothing. Death and life are one. The connections we share extend past our physical selves and time. In vibrating with the universe, we do not cling to imaginations of faith.

The human quest should be one of courage. To exist in the living form is to carry the consciousness in recycled and reconstructed materials governed by the other universal forces. But in its truest form, consciousness is free and pervasive. When our physical body dies, the consciousness that is trapped within is set free. So to die is to be free, to be born is to become captive. Why then do we celebrate birth and mourn death? Should it not be the other way around. It is akin to prisoners celebrating the arrival of new prisoners into their facility. To be a prisoner is to suffer. To tie ourselves to the prison with wants and needs and comparisons is suffering.

The mind is a temporary space that is connected at the collision of the physical being and the conscious self, and it serves to liaison the two. Yet, the mind tames the consciousness, quoting the need for the physical being's survival. The body strives, the mind sees and strives, but the consciousness simply is. Realization is the knowing that the striving does not need to happen, that the mind need not protect the body, and that the true objective, with or without this physical self, is the bliss of the consciousness vibrating freely.

A realized person has no teachings to give, no new ideas to share. What new ideas can be invented when all that needs to be known is already known? Perhaps the realized being can communicate that the truths are there- waiting to be dug up and seen, but they do not communicate this in words. Presence and energy are all that is needed. If the seeker of truths is ready, they will sense the vibrations and spontaneously remove the blocks that prevent the vibrations of the conscious."

What Krishna says is true. But it is difficult for me to accept it.

After all, the idea of a God outside of me in one form or another, has held me together all these years.

It is difficult to substitute faith with philosophy. But truth, once I know is out there, will find a way to seep in. It is only a question of time.

Chapter Fifteen

Riva

I first see Riva in the communal dining hall. She is one of
the few foreigners in the Ashram. The communal hall is
a place for silence. We serve food and eat food in silence.
Women and Men sit on opposite sides of the hall. So there
is very little mingling that happens during eating times.

I notice Riva right away- she is tall and thin, has braided
golden hair and blue eyes, her pale skin mismatched to
the orange salwar and vermillion on her forehead. She is
serving rice, going from one person to the next, a bright
smile radiating her face. She notices me staring at her. She
smiles. She is probably used to people staring at a white
woman in sanyasin (renunciate) clothes. I smile back. I
continue thinking about her after dinner. I realize why she
stands out in my eyes. She reminds me of Alice.

I keep bumping into Riva as I go about the campus activities
with Karna. She is always smiling, always happy. After
two years on the road, I am suddenly thinking about my
appearance. I shaved my head and facial hair the very first
day I had come to the Ashram. I look at myself in the

bathroom mirror. Chronic hunger has given my eyes an unnatural gleam. My cheekbones are jutting out. Two of my lower teeth are missing- courtesy of a policeman who decided to kick them in.

I feel self-conscious for no reason.

Karna is a simple soul. He is not weighed down by the grand happiness and sufferings of the world. He is not ambitious for his voice to be heard or his actions to be seen. What need or pain he sees in front of him, he addresses them fearlessly and without judgment. When he feels he has done what he can, he moves on. He sees no need for philosophies of heaven and hell. Maybe that is why he sleeps peacefully at night.

I see him as the brother I never had. I believe he too sees me as a younger brother.

Prem Baba is a constant presence. I see him at the weekly Darshans and sometimes when he comes out to stroll in the vast agricultural land that belongs to the Ashram. Whenever Baba asks Karna to meet him, I tag along. Baba sends Karna out on missions- to 'rescue' people in difficult circumstances and bring them to the Ashram, just as had happened to me. Karna is always thrilled to do this. Sometimes he comes back empty-handed. Sometimes he has people accompanying him. The people who come often stay for a short time and leave. But a few like me, stay on to serve.

Karna and I work in the garden, along with several other volunteers. Working with plants is a healing experience. It is beautiful to see the seeds we planted become vegetables and fruits, which become part of our consumption. The labor keeps me away from my dark thoughts. Plus the company of Karna brightens even my most difficult days.

I trust Karna enough to tell him my life story- of my journeys from Chennai to the US and back, of Alice and Sita, of my inner darkness. He listens wide-eyed.

"I always knew you were more than what you appear to be Arjuna," he says with wonderment. "You should be doing so much more with your life!"

But he does not push me.

I ask Karna to not share my story with anyone.

He agrees.

Karna seems a bit agitated one day.

"I broke my promise," he says with anguish. 'I was talking to Riva. She was asking about you, and without thinking I shared your life story with her."

I am confused.

Why was Riva asking about me? It had become a routine for us to smile at each other in the lunch hall. Once or twice, I had interacted with her when I brought in the produce from the fields to the kitchen where she volunteers. I cannot help thinking how much she looks like Alice.

"It is okay Karna. What was she asking about me?"

Karna seems relieved.

"Oh just that she was curious about you and what your story was."

I realize I don't know anything about Riva.

Karna reads my mind.

"Riva is from Israel. She was on a sightseeing tour last year when she saw Prem Baba's book in a bookstall in Hyderabad. She left her traveling troupe and headed over here. You see, she was working her way through a divorce. I guess Baba's words brought her peace."

After a very long time, I feel something shifting inside. I cannot place my finger on it.

Six months have gone by since I came to the Ashram.

Karna is out on one of his 'rescue missions'.

The Ashram usually shuts down by 8 pm. It is now past midnight. For some reason, I cannot sleep. I decide to step outside the walls of my volunteer's quarters for some fresh air. I stop. Someone is sobbing under the large peepul tree in the backyard. I rush over. It is Riva. She is sitting on a pile of stones. It is a beautiful full-moon night. I can see her hair is disheveled.

"What is wrong Riva?"

She bursts out into a muffled wail.

"Please help me!" she pleads.

"What happened?"

I panic.

"Prem Baba raped me..."

"What?!"

Between her sobs, she tells me that she had approached Prem Baba to initiate her into the path of sanyasin. Prem Baba had asked her to come late in the evening to his quarters. There he had raped her. And threatened to have her eliminated if she disclosed it to anyone.

I am shocked by the gravity of her exposition.

"The Baba did this?"

The first thought that came to my mind, for some reason, was Karna. He is going to be devastated if he comes to know what his master has done.

"Let's go to the police station," I whisper hurriedly.

"That's no use. All the police and politicians are under his influence."

I remember that Baba's influence crawls deep into power structures.

"Let's go to the Israeli embassy then. Surely they can help."

"Baba and his men have taken my passport and visa and everything I own. I do not have a rupee in my hand."

She sobs uncontrollably again.

"And I do not think it will help to talk about what happened to the Ashram community. He said he would frame me for thieving and have me arrested. I am stuck. I just want to go home!"

I gather the courage to reach out and hold her quivering hands in mine.

"Riva. Please don't lose heart. I am going to find a way."

My brain is racing to find a way. How I wish Karna was here. All Riva needed was a few thousand rupees to get to the Israeli embassy in New Delhi. It would be a long journey by train and some more. But I knew that she would find support, even without her passport or visa. I know where to get this money.

"Wait here Riva. I will be back."

There is an offertory in the main hall of the Ashram next to the marble statues of the Gods. It is emptied every couple of days. If I am lucky, there is still money in the offertory. Karna, as one of the dedicated members of the Ashram, has the keys to the main hall. In addition to garden work, he cleans the main hall. I rush back to our volunteer quarters where Karna and I share a room. I dig through his belongings until I find the keys. As quietly as I can I slink my way into the main hall. I know full well that Baba's lieutenants will beat me to a pulp if they catch me, and then hand me over to the police. But all I can think of now is this sobbing girl with golden hair, who reminds me so much of another that I loved so, so long ago.

Fate is on my side. No one is awake. I make my way to the
offertory. It is a wooden box with a flimsy lock, mounted on
a marble stand. A heavy incense holder next to a God assists
me in breaking the lock. There is money- lots of it. I grab
everything and run out of the place.

Riva is still where I left her under the Peepul tree.

"Come, come with me. We must leave this place."

She trusts me enough to follow. We quickly exit the Ashram
compound and rush into the night.

I am praying that no one has noticed.

The railway station is not far away.

After an hour of hustled walk, we arrive at the station. I buy
two tickets to New Delhi and go to the train platform. With
our saffron clothes and tousled hair, it would be difficult to
remain inconspicuous on the almost empty platform.

The minutes tick by slowly. I look around expecting
someone from the Ashram to run in and get us. No one
comes but I have a bad feeling brewing in my stomach. I
give Riva half the loot from the temple offertory.

"Keep this," I tell her. "It should take you to the embassy
should something happen."

"You are coming with me, arent you?" she pleads.

"Yes, but you keep this money"

It is almost an hour before the train arrives. We get on the
train and find a quiet corner. I am desperately counting the
minutes for the train to leave the station.

I hear a commotion outside. I carefully peep through the window of the train.

A couple of men from Baba's ashram, along with a policeman are going from compartment to compartment, climbing in checking, and moving on to the next, noisily barking their observations to each other...

My heart is thumping. It is a race against time. If the train starts moving before they reach our compartment, they will have to disembark and we will be free.

Three... two.... They are only two compartments away from where Riva and I are hiding. The train is showing no signs of starting.

I make up my mind.

"Riva. Just stay here. Do not move whatever happens. Please leave India and never come back."

She reaches out to me, confused, trying to understand the situation.

"Hide!" I hiss. And then I sneak out of the train compartment and begin to run. I am not trying to hide. I just want to give enough time in the chase so that the train can start and Riva can be safe.

As I run, I hear a shout. One of the Ashram men has spotted me.

I look back to see the two ashram men and the policeman running behind me.

I run up the stairs leading outside to the entrance of the station. I am surprised at how fast I can run.

From the corner of my eye, I see the train for Delhi leaving the platform.

I smile even as I run.

Riva is safe.

They tie me to a pole in a dark unused room of the temple and beat me up all the way into the morning.

Even for my body used to abuse, the pain is unbearable.

But an even bigger fear looms in my mind.

If they hand me to the police and the police find out about the incident with Sita...

The door crashes open.

Karna is standing there with one of Baba's lieutenants.

"Here is the mother*** you brought into the ashram. He stole money from God and eloped with a woman"

Even in the dim light, I can see the anger and disappointment in Karna's eyes.

"If you wanted money..." he begins

"Karna," I whimper "Baba raped Riva. I helped her escape"

Karna gasps. Baba's lieutenant crashes his shoes on my face.

"How dare you speak ill of Baba!"

He punches me again.

Karna slaps me across my face.

"Don't you dare speak ill of my master!" he hisses angrily.

"Tell us where that whore is. Did she get on the train?" the lieutenant asks me. Then he turns to Karna. "The two idiots who went to the railway station did not know they were supposed to be looking for Riva as well."

I am silently grateful for running out of the train compartment when I did. I am horrified to imagine Riva in my current state.

"Talk to him. If he cannot tell us where Riva is headed, then by evening we will have him at the police station. We have the cc TV recording of him stealing from the offertory. He will not stay quiet with police treatment."

More than the physical pain, it hurts me to lose the trust of the one person I saw as my own brother.

It is dark by the time they take me to the Police station. All this happens without raising hullabaloo at the ashram. Very likely Baba is giving a sermon about how he has forgiven two misguided devotees who stole from the temple and eloped.

I am booked and sent into a holding jail. The fireworks would start when the inspector would come in the morning.

Around midnight, someone opens my jail cell.

It is the head constable. He is the one who brought me in from the ashram.

He is an old man with a wrinkled face. He somehow seems very familiar.

He thrusts a folded envelope into my hands.

"Quick, the station cameras are off. There is an autorickshaw at the end of the road. I have already paid him. He will drop you off in Vizag. Take a bus and leave this state and don't come back."

I am dazed and shocked at this sudden turn of events.

"Leave now," he whispers firmly.

I do not wait to ask questions. I follow the head constable to the back door and climb over a small wall and get to the street. I run to the end of the street where an autorickshaw is waiting in the shadows. I climb in, and like clockwork, the autorickshaw driver leaves the place. We ride through the night.

When I calm down a little, I open the envelope that the head constable had given me.

Inside are a few two-thousand rupee notes and a letter.

'My dear Arjuna, I am sorry for slapping you today. That was the only way I could not raise suspicion. I am unable to believe that my guru would hurt anyone. I also refuse to believe that you are a thief. I have only seen goodness and gentleness in you in all the time we were blessed to be together. I can only surmise that there is

some misunderstanding. But we cannot wait to resolve the truth now. That is why I have asked my father to let you out of jail. He is doing it for me, at great risk to his job and reputation. But he loves me much. Please take this money and take a train from Vizag to Banaras. There, seek out a dear old friend of mine. His name is Ramdas Baba. He is an aghori sadhu. Tell him that I sent you. He will help you. I wish we did not have to part this way.

May the Gods be with you, my brother.

~ Karna'

I suddenly realize why the head constable's face seemed so familiar to me.

Tears flow uncontrollably from my eyes- this time in gratitude for the love of a true friend.

The auto reaches Vizag early in the morning.

The man drops me off outside the railway station and leaves.

I get a train for the holy city of Banaras.

I know I will dare not come back to this part of India again.

And I am already missing Karna.

Chapter Sixteen

Reflections in the Cave: Freedom

Today, I listen to Krishna's reflections on freedom.

'When I free my mind from the binds of conditioning, I become liberated

When I free myself from my mind, I become enlightened

True freedom is freedom from identities.

You are not anyone's son or daughter

Neither strong nor weak

Not a man or woman or child

You are no one's friend or enemy

You are not your memories or your knowing

You are not your mind

The air makes the balloon float

But the air is not the balloon

Even time is not your captor

The beginning and the end of the universe are within you

You have partaken of every moment of consciousness that has been and will be

So

Why not choose to be free?

The eternal timeless spirit is a prisoner of the mind and body, having lost its ability to gaze through the multiple dimensions of its being, save through the narrow windows of dreams.

Yet, within this prison man hopes for freedom.

He hopes that wealth and fame will gain him freedom when all they bring are burdens and ties. The harder he strives to break free, the more walls he builds around himself. This is the paradox of freedom. The ones that can get closest to the window and gaze at the bird flying beyond the prison walls, awaiting their turn to soar, are the ones who have disburdened themselves of the effort to be free. In losing the desire for freedom, they gain freedom. In snapping off their wings of striving, they soar.

Freedom is a choice I make.

My room is soggy and filthy. All the leftovers from countless meals are putrefying, festering with worms. Yes, It stinks. I have been hoarding, afraid to let go. I also know I need to open the doors to let the air in and let the stink out. I must make sure I put up a net so the flies do not come in and add to the decay. And I must work hard to clean my room. I know this is what I should do. But it is too much work and I am afraid of throwing away the trash. I have become too comfortable with it. The trash and stink have become a part of my identity. I have a choice. I can stay here with the trash and suffer. Or I can open the doors, and start cleaning, so I can experience the blossoms of flowers.

Yes, freedom is a choice I make'

Chapter Seventeen

The Way of the Aghori

My body is still throbbing with pain from the beating when the train reaches Varanasi in the early hours of the morning. I hobble out of the train station, scarred by the experiences of the previous day, but grateful for the way things turned out. I am thinking of Riva and Karna. I hope Karna or his dad do not get into trouble because of me. I also hope that Riva has found her way to the Israeli embassy and that she will safely find her way home.

Hinduism has seven sacred cities. Varanasi is the holiest among them. It is believed that Shiva, the god of destruction, won a fight against Brahma, the five-headed creator of the universe. Having cut off one of the heads of Brahma, Shiva walked the universe with pride. When he came to Varanasi however, Brahma's head fell off Shiva's hands and disappeared into the ground. And so the land became forever hallowed. If God can lose his ego here, so can man.

My senses are in overdrive as I step out of the train station into the thronging rush of life in Varanasi. I stop by one of the many roadside shops to satiate my raging hunger and find a shop selling cheap saffron clothes. I ask the shopkeeper if there is some way I can find a holy man, a sadhu, in Varanasi.

He laughs.

"This city has 23000 temples," he says, "there are probably a hundred thousand sadhus on the streets. It will be easier for you to find a pin in a haystack."

He sees my crestfallen face.

"What is this sadhu's name? The one you seek?"

"Ramdass Baba. He is an aghori."

"Ah, that might make things a little simpler. Although it is still a crazy venture, there are fewer aghori babas than other sadhus. But the problem is, one can never really say who is a true aghori."

I had heard about aghoris before, but I have never met one. This fierce and mysterious sect chooses to pursue enlightenment in a radically different way than the rest of the renunciates. They opt for the shortcut- the dark and scary paths- that challenge sanity and break all notions of duality. An aghori sees no right and wrong, pure and impure. Everything is good and a manifestation of the divine. So they see that their role is to break past the biases and taboos that have been created by the mind. And in so doing they break the illusion of duality and access their own divine nature. I have heard of some horrific stories about the extent to which an aghori may go to, to break the biases of his mind. I have heard stories of aghoris consuming stuff that others find revolting, even feces, urine, and decaying human flesh. I have heard that they eat out of human skulls and sleep with corpses and use mind-altering drugs. I wonder if Ramdass Baba, if I ever find him, would be this way, and it scares me. I consider not seeking out Ramdass Baba, but it is easier to believe Karna.

"Go to Ravindrapuri," the shopkeeper advises me, 'and find Baba Keenaram Sthal, the headquarters of the Aghora sect. If the one you seek is an aghora you may find some leads there."

Some people consider the 16th-century spiritual master, Baba Keenaram, the founder of the aghora sect. I make inquiries about Ramdass Baba, but do not find the one I seek. I am a mendicant. I have lived this way for a long time now. I am not in a rush to meet him.

Ten days in, I am still getting used to this fascinating city- the noise, the smells, the breathtaking religious rituals in the evenings. The shopkeeper was not exaggerating. Everywhere I turn, there is a temple or a mosque. I also see an industry built around spirituality. Tourists who are willing to pay money to take pictures with 'holy men' of Varanasi, and men who groom to play the part of a sadhu to eke out a living.

The majority of sadhus I have met have at some point in their life experienced a spiritual calling, even if it meant for a short period. Oftentimes this spiritual calling happened in response to adverse life events, an escape from immediate suffering. But after a while, the spark is gone, but they stay around because there is no other destination. For these people, the sadhu lifestyle means inclusion into a community of people who find joy in semi-detachment. The garb offers them identities, liberties, and respect that they otherwise would not receive. Without a barrier for entry, anyone can don the garb and become a renunciate, although their initial burst of spiritual seeking fizzles out very soon until only rituals remain. And then there are a few like Prem Baba, whose only objective seemed to be to manipulate others for money, power, and sexual favors.

My body has healed quite well from the beatings. I hang out near the ghats, the stone stairs on the banks of the Ganges river, or near Baba Keenaram Sthal, living my old beggar's life, this time in saffron clothes.

One of the late evenings I am roughly woken up from a half-sleep. A man in his late thirties, half-naked body covered in crematorial ash, with piercing eyes, dreadlocks bunched over his head and a long disheveled beard, layers of beads hanging around his neck.

"Are you looking for me?" he asks me curtly.

"Are you Ramdass Baba?"

"Depends on who is asking"

"My name is Arjuna. Karna from Haripuram, sent me to you."

The stern face blossoms into a broad smile. The transformation is beautiful.

"That bastard has sent you," he says with obvious elation. "How is he? Still slaving away to that mother**** Prem Baba?"

The suddenness of this colorful language, coming from a man in holy garb, catches me unprepared. I begin to laugh.

"Come with me," he says, "we must talk."

Sitting at the steps of a crematorial ghat, I tell Ramdass about my journeys. He listens, eyes half-closed, smoking on his chillum (smoking pipe), occasionally interrupting me with a cough or a chant. When I finish, I am not sure if Ramdass is awake or asleep.

It is my turn to ask him his story.

"Oh, Karna didn't tell you? We were three of us, me, him, and another bastard Rajam. We drank, gambled, and wreaked havoc in our town. One day Rajam got sick, started throwing up blood. Doctor said he had drunk too much and his liver was bust. He died in our arms. His parents and ours cursed us out and blamed us for his death. Watching him die like that got to both of us. Karna found a pamphlet about Prem Baba and attended one of his meetings and decided to stay. I went too, but I did not like the looks of that man. I told Karna straight up that Prem Baba was a cheat. But he disagreed. I wandered around the town for a little longer. Then I heard about aghoris from a wandering sadhu and came to Varanasi. And I have been here since."

He stares at me in silence.

"Ok, so you are here now. What does he want me to do with you?"

I shrug. I have no idea. I tell him so.

He laughs.

"No idea is good. No destination is good. This is a big city. There is place for you too. Hang around. If I am around you can hang around with me. If I am not there, you are no stranger to this lifestyle. If you ask me for help, I will help you if I can, if not I will tell you to go screw yourself. Either way, you will not go hungry in Varanasi."

Chapter Eighteen

Reflections in the Cave: Compassion

I put the last set of batteries into the cassette player. When these batteries run out, I will only have the memories of Krishna's recordings. Of course, the person behind the recordings is still with me, and his voice echoes in my mind.

If I stand in front of a waterfall with a tiny cup

Hoping that the larger the waterfall the more water I will carry away with me

Would I succeed?

Should not my goal be to make my cup bigger

Not seek bigger waterfalls?

If I read a thousand books and listen to a thousand discourses

and yet my mind and heart be puny

What would I gain?

Surrounding myself with more does not mean I can consume more.

Consuming more may not make me happier.

Knowing what makes me happy and doing what makes me happy is all that matters.

When I stop comparisons I realize how little I actually need.

And so I pray that every day I may:

learn to leave room for want.

learn to resist the temptation to be full.

learn not to overfill myself with good things.

learn to always remain a little hungry and a little poorer than my means.

And this way, I will remain awake to others' pain

And compassion will become possible.'

I think about the day Krishna and I first met on my path to Bhairav jhamp. He saw a suffering being, and chose not to ignore its suffering. He felt the pain of this stranger and jumped in, going so far as to invite me into his personal space so I can heal. I wonder how much hunger this man must carry to have so much compassion for another.

I carry forward this conversation to our evening tea.

"We are all born compassionate, Arjuna," Krishna says sipping tea. Today is extra special because, for no specific reason, we opened up a can of condensed milk and added liberal amounts of it to our chai.

"When we leave out the fear, see that we are all one life in many bodies, when we realize that one cannot be truly happy when someone else suffers, that we cannot find pleasure at the cost of someone else, compassion becomes the only real path forward. But how we complicate life with our stories. This earth has so much abundance. We need to remember that this is an abundant world, we can all have everything that matters, and never be lesser because of it."

His words are simple and profound. They touch a chord deep in me. I realize compassion as the end of suffering-mine, and others. I need to start by erasing some stories within.

Chapter Nineteen

Mother

It has been a year since I arrived here in Varanasi. I have
become part of the landscape. Sleeping on the ghats and
waking up to the noise and commotion of this holy chaos,
I am no longer alone. There are hundreds of mendicants
like me who call the banks of the Ganga their own. I am also
now an accepted part of the Aghora community, thanks to
Ramdass, with whom I have been tagging along since the
day I met him. He goes away often to the mountains, and
in those days I hang out in any of the scores of ghats.

People come from all over to cleanse their sins here, and in
that state of mind, they are generous to the ones in saffron.
There are two major ghats dedicated to cremation. The
air here has a permanent tinge of burning flesh. People
bring their dead to be burned on the raised stone slabs.
Everyone is in a rush to send their ones on the path
to heaven. It is a profitable business for the people who
run the cremation and the demand is high. The poorer
people, who cannot afford the cremation on the ghats,
simply cover the dead in a shroud and toss them into
the holy river. If the river is purifying the sins of her
people, people are not doing anything to purify the river.
A sickly silver sheen permanently coats the surface of the

water, with an occasional corpse peeping out on the surface. The numerous stray dogs drag the decaying corpses into the small islands in the river. The best-lived lives end up here as half-burnt flesh and food for hungry dogs. This is the reality that the ones who come here seek permanent liberation from. Curiously no one seems to care. What we experience every day becomes our norm. In fact just a ghat away, the living bathe in droves, oblivious to the death downstream. After all, one dip in the holiest river in the world can wash away the karma of a lifetime.

I have become accustomed to watching decomposing flesh and half-burned body parts stick out of burning wood. It used to revolt me. It does not anymore. Some of the aghori babas I hang out with tell me that they have eaten the flesh of decaying corpses as a way to break past the dualities of acceptable and taboo. I have seen them meditate on bodies of the recently dead, hoping to tap into the remaining energy of life before it dissipates into the universe. I hear of other tantric practices that make my toes curl. Ramdass sometimes suggests that I consider becoming initiated. As much as I see the truth in transgressing boundaries and biases to access the God within, I am hesitant to cross over. Crossing over, for me, I feel will be a point of no return. I am scared of being restricted inside a circle I cannot step out of.

I hang out with Aghoris in the evenings, smoking weed in my chillum (yes, I have obtained one now), escaping into alternative realities shrouded behind the dense smoke. These evenings are a brotherhood of stories, some religious, some philosophical, some gruesome. Ours is a motley crowd of people who have sought to escape the well-worn path, impatient for a spiritual shortcut, with inspired starts and now likely caught in tedious callousness.

I have stopped thinking about my journeys, mostly. The endless nights of smoking cannabis and the non-stop unfolding of life and death in front of my eyes have made me numb to my own suffering. I am in the middle of a bubble that I care not to pop. I simply do not care.

Next to Manikarna ghat, the largest of the crematorial ghats is a home where the dying come to die. The dying and their family check in to the Azadi home, are given 15 days to die or check out. And when the death happens, the bodies are brought across the road to be cremated.

This morning I sit in a narrow lane leading to the ghat watching the people come and go through the gates. The higher caste dead and the lower caste dead get to be cremated in different parts of the ghat. Caste follows the dead even to the cremation grounds.

The sun is shining brightly in my eyes as I watch an old man's body being brought into the ghat by hired bearers. An old woman, likely his wife, is teetering along at the end of the procession. She stops outside the cremation grounds. Women are not allowed in. A younger man goes into the cremation grounds with the body to perform the last rites.

The old lady turns away from the ghat and sits on a stone not far from where I am. I squint to look at her. I can see her face more clearly now.

My heart stops.

My mother!

I am looking at the face of my mother. She has aged many decades but...

but my mother is dead.

I get up and walk over to her. My body is shaking as I come closer to the old woman.

Yes. It is not my mother.

But it very well could have been.

The last I had seen my mother was ten years ago at the airport when I left for the US to study. I had planned to save up money and return to India in two years, at the end of my master's program. But then, Alice happened. And my mother had died a year later.

I look keenly at the old woman in front of me. She is not crying, but I see great sadness on her face. She rises up to bow to me. I realize I am still in the garb of a sadhu. And I have ash smeared all across my face and body. She does not sense the struggling human behind this costume.

"Please sit, Mataji," I say gently, grasping her hands.

She does.

"Was that your husband?" I ask, pointing to the ghat.

"Yes," her voice trembles. "Please pray for him Swamiji."

I am no spiritual master. But I have learned a few mantras listening to Ramdass. I repeat them with closed eyes. It seems to give her some comfort.

"Is that your son? The one who went in?"

"No. That is my nephew. My son is in the US, married, settled with his wife and children. Too important to even come down for his own father's cremation." she begins to weep. Her face shrivels in pain.

"We loved him so much, our only son. Everything we did, we did for him. But now that he has everything, he has ignored us. Like dirty laundry. We did not want his money. We do not want anything from him. Just for him to be there in our last hours. My husband and I came to the Azadi home seven days ago with my nephew. All the time, my husband kept looking at the door of our room, hoping that our son would somehow walk in through the door. But our son did not come... my husband died uttering his name."

As she narrates her pain, I feel like a searing rod has been thrust through my heart.

This would have been my mother on her deathbed. Waiting for her only son who would never come. How she must have suffered.

A wall, built over years of self-loathing, and now becoming coated with apathy, has begun to crack.

I too, begin to sob.

"Mataji, I will pray for you and your son. I hope you reconcile and find peace."

There is no greater suffering than what happens inside the contours of the mind.

I have spent years wallowing in my guilt and regret, wishing I could go back to all the points in my path where I took the wrong turn. I did not realize that I had made all of this suffering about me. Today, the old woman has shattered my shell of self-pity.

I am confronting my regrets through the eyes of the one who has suffered through me. I live through the last minutes of my mother on her deathbed staring at the open door waiting for me to come, I experience the helpless pain of Alice watching her husband devolve into a tormentor and alcoholic, I endure the agony of Alice's parents as they bury their only beloved daughter in the prime of her life...

I cannot find words to describe the intensity of self-loathing and hate I feel for myself.

Ramdass returns from his travels that night.

He finds me in a dark corner of an alley near Manikarna ghat, shivering in the November cold, where I met the old lady.

Through the day and evening, one thing has become clear to me: I cannot continue to live on this way- a worthless excuse of creation worming through life spewing suffering everywhere I go.

Ramdass is a good man. But he is not the best listener. I try to communicate my suffering to him. He listens for a little while and offers me some hash to smoke. Perhaps my suffering is trivial compared to the things he has seen and experienced as an Aghori. He tells me pain is temporary. If I can numb my pain now, I will be ready to move on in the morning. I reluctantly take a puff, then throw up all over myself.

"Ram," I ask quietly, "the pain burns me alive. If I give up my life today, here by the holy river, would I get the hope of escaping this pain forever?"

He looks at me quizzically. He never shies away from conversations on death.

"You mean, if you kill yourself? Commit suicide?"

I nod my head.

He thinks for a while.

"You know, in the Garuda Purana, it is said that if one has committed a grave sin such as murder or rape, and if that person feels guilt and remorse, he is allowed to commit suicide as a way of self-punishment. Such a form of self-punishment will free them from the Karma of their lifetime."

He looks at me.

"I know you have committed a grave sin, and you feel great remorse. In fact, you are living through hell while still on earth. As an Aghori, I find no harm in you seeking liberation from this suffering."

He takes a few more puffs from his chillum.

"However, Varanasi is not the place for you to give up the claim over your life. This is a place only for those who are leaving their bodily ties the natural way."

"Where else then?"

"There is a place in the mountains near the Kedarnath temple. Bhairav jhamp... People jump off the mountains to sever their ties to this life and to reincarnation. It is not easy to find the spot, but it exists. If it is your destiny to escape reincarnation there, you will find the way."

I had heard of Kedarnath before- the place of salvation high up in the mountains.

I urge Ramdass to tell me more. He shares what he knows.

"Kedarnath may already be closed for winter,' he adds. 'The snow makes it impossible to go up and down the mountain. You can try to go there now, but it is likely the road to the temple may already be blocked. If you want to go, take the train to Haridwar tomorrow morning. There are some connecting buses that will take you to Gaurikund."

He closes his eyes and says a little prayer for me.

"If I don't see you on this side of life,' he says matter of factly, "may Kala Bhairava guide your way."

He takes a couple more puffs from his chillum, smiles at me, gets up, and walks away.

His utter lack of emotion at my imminent suicide jars me even in the middle of my tattered mindset. I tell myself that is the way of the aghora.

The next morning, I buy a ticket to Haridwar and begin my journey to Kedarnath.

I tell myself this would be my final farewell.

But it was not.

Because I met Krishna, and followed him to his cave.

Chapter Twenty

Rebirth

It is February here in Kedarnath. The snow has been falling non-stop for days. It is the coldest it has been since I arrived here.

The fever starts during the night.

My body quakes with an intensity of pain that I cannot remember experiencing before. Every cell of my body burns. As I weave in and out of consciousness, I see Krishna next to me, patting my burning forehead with cold cloth. I scream and writhe in agony. My screaming becomes part of my febrile dreaming. It takes many eons for that night to pass. When the morning comes, I am immobile.

And it is not just my body that is in agony.

For much of three years I had eaten and drunk filth that no human should. I had been punched and beaten up, had become emaciated with hunger, and scabbed with maggoty wounds. For most of those three years, I had lived the life of a repulsive street cur- clothes tattered, hair matted and filled with lice, sleeping amidst bandicoots and scorpions. Yet, something had me sewn together.

But that now seems to be falling apart.

Just when life is providing me an opportunity for healing, my body and spirit are deciding to give up.

I do not have the energy to fight anymore.

I am finally ready to die. I should have died a long time ago when Alice and my baby died.

Perhaps sticking around so long was my biggest mistake.

Perhaps all this wandering and pain was my deserved punishment for my sins.

And now I feel I have suffered enough, paid my dues.

The throbbing incessant pain of my being will come to an end, and I will find peace.

Krishna tells me it has been a week, but to me, it seems much longer.

Slowly, very slowly, movement returns to my limbs.

I am able to prop myself against the walls of the cave and hold my head up straight, albeit with much effort. Through the day Krishna tends to me, feeding and cleaning with the loving tenderness of a mother. He braves the frigid February snow to wash and dry my soiled clothes, cooks gruel over the fire, and feeds me in small spoonfuls even as I cough and sputter with each intake.

All the while, I see no signs of complaint from Krishna.

His winter would have been, like the many years before it, a time of quietude and meditation if not for me. I had come crashing into his life, burrowing into his meager resources, dampening his spirit with my brokenness, and offering nothing in return. And now I was tasking him to be my caregiver.

In my helplessness and pain, I am filled with a revolting hatred for my putrid existence.

I wake up in the night remembering a long-forgotten story.

King Lavana, the great king of UttaraPandava, has everything he can ask for- wealth, respect, health, love. One day, an ascetic comes into his parlor and waves a wand. In an instant, the king is transported to a dry forest with no sign of life. For days, the king wanders the arid land searching for water and food and a way back home. At the very door of death, a forest woman, a woodcutter's daughter rescues him. Bound by his promise to marry her in exchange for life-saving food, and finding no way back home, he becomes a woodcutter. Burdened with a cruel wife and callous sons, Lavana still manages to perform his duties to his trade and family life. Then a great famine strikes the land, and his first two sons abandon him. Carrying his youngest son and his complaining wife, he treks across the land seeking greener land. After days, realizing that his child and wife would die without food, he walks away to a clearing and makes a fire. He tells his wife and child that they should return to the fire in an hour and they would find food and that after eating they should carry on without him. After they leave, Lavana prepares to jump into the fire, and watching the swirling flames he remembers that many many years ago he was a King. He remembers that he had a wife that loved him, children that adored him, subjects who respected him, and enemies that feared him. With one great sigh for a lost past, Lavana jumps into the scorching flames *and wakes up in his parlor*. To his great surprise, his minister tells him that he had appeared to fall asleep for only a minute. Lavana realizes that he had lived an entire lifetime in a minute of his dreaming.

And the ascetic who had sent him on his journey was nowhere to be found.

I wake up wondering what it would be like if I closed my eyes and died to this reality. I hope that I will wake up on a soft bed next to a girl with golden hair and tell her tales about a long and horrid dream I had.

But my reality is this cave on the top of a mountain, and the girl with the golden hair is long gone.

I sob uncontrollably. The tears do not cool my skin burning with fever.

Krishna takes the end of his shoulder towel and tenderly wipes my tears.

In that moment I see my own mother in this old man.

She used to wipe away my tears with the loose end of her saree.

I too was a king.

I was loved. I loved.

"Why Krishna? Why do I have to live this wretched life? I should have died a long time ago with Alice and my baby. But here I am, in this miserable excuse of a life, living in endless moments of agony"

I am crying hard now.

Krishna does not reply immediately

"I wish I could tell you I know why life happens the way it happens. So many things in life we have no control over. But inner peace, which you so desperately need now, is in your control"

I do not feel in control of anything. Not at this moment. I let him know so.

"I am not asking you to deny your pain. I am only urging you to remember you have a choice to forgive yourself and move on"

"How can I forgive myself, Krishna. Every minute I close my eyes I remember Alice, my baby, my parents, all the wrong choices I made."

Krishna places his hands over my throbbing head. I feel his healing flow through me.

"Yes, it is impossible to not remember," he replies gently. "But...to forgive does not mean to forget. To forgive is to let go of the emotion, to forget is to let go of the lesson. When we forget the experience, we may be forced to learn our lessons all over again.

So we must remember, if only so we do not repeat the experience.

But to remember does not mean that we suffer the emotions of bitter experiences over and over. To suffer for a past you cannot change, or to let go and be free, is a choice you make.

Yes, Arjuna, you have made many mistakes. You have hurt people and people have hurt you. That is the truth. But it is a truth of the past. For all your remembering you cannot go back and change a single thing. What happened, happened. Why? No one knows. That was how life scripted your story. Either you accept your past, learn from your mistakes and move forward a little bit wiser, or be chained to your past and continue the suffering. I hope you choose to let go and be free.

To forgive is to choose freedom- freedom not from memories, but from the emotional baggage of what cannot be changed.

I hope someday you can look at your journeys as you would watch a movie- appreciating the beauty of the script, knowing fully well that what happens on the screen is not for change."

"You are an enlighted being Krishna," I counter, "all this is easy for you. But I am an ordinary man. I am one of the billions that journey through life in tiny intervals of days and nights, sorrows and laughter. To remember without feeling pain is not easy for the likes of me."

"You say that, Arjuna. Yet you hunger for freedom from pain. If at this moment you choose freedom and peace, if you desire it with all your heart and soul, it is yours. No one is standing between your freedom and you except your own mind. If you choose, you are free."

"But how? Where do I start? I am weak and the darkness overpowers any hope of light."

"The moment you unequivocally dedicate yourself to freedom, you will feel a veil lift. You will realize that you no longer have to chase doors because you will find yourself standing in a place without walls. This is the beauty of the mind. With one second of intent, you break down years of sorrow. This is free will."

"If life was the author of my script, the script she has written for me is wantonly cruel."

I can see Krishna smile faintly.

"Perhaps. But the script she has written for you is brilliant nonetheless. Look at the loose ends of your life Arjuna and see the magnificent pattern that has emerged. You caused the death of Alice, but you saved Riva. Your unborn daughter died because of you, but you protected Sita. You were not there for your father in his old age, but you held space for a dying man in his last breath. Everything in your life has come full circle. You have found redemption through your choices."

He pauses and removes the fevered cloth from my forehead, so he can dip it in cold water. Then he wrings it and reapplies it on my forehead.

As he speaks, the throbbing pain in my body begins to subside.

"Do you know what happens inside a pupa, Arjuna? It is not a pretty sight. The caterpillar has to digest itself and become a protein soup before the remaining cells rebuild into the beautiful butterfly. What survives disaster feeds on the remains to create wings. I want you to recognize that you are a pupa in the final stages of your transformation into a beautiful butterfly.

Arjuna, when you come out of this, I want you to be able to visit your memories whenever you wish without fear and the burden of sorrow. But you must make that decision. You must accept that the past cannot be changed. And you must choose to dream of a future without the baggage of the past. Forgiveness is not an incident, it is a mindset. Even if you choose happiness now, shame and regret, and guilt will find ways to sneak into your mind, in your moments of weakness. The forgiving mind is a sword sharpened in times of peace so it is ready to be wielded in the dark times.

So, start with awareness. In every possible opportunity, tell yourself this: 'I am simply an actor in life's script. The sole purpose of my past is so I learn not to impose any more suffering upon myself and others in what lies ahead. 'So much of the hard work happens not when we are chained by guilt and angst, but in the times when our minds are free and at ease. Be simple and be honest with yourself. Accept every day as it comes to you with gratitude. Know that your role is to act and learn not to become tethered to the outcomes of your actions. Live no more than a single day at a time. Today well lived takes care of tomorrow. *And trust the script of life.*

When the leftover seeds of past hurts have no nourishment or reinforcement coming in, they will starve and die. In their place, flowers will grow. Your inner world will blossom and you will know freedom. With tiny choices every day, you will find peace."

He pauses and strokes my head some more.

" But now, simply rest. Ask no more questions. Seek no more answers. Simply heal. You will find time to reflect and find your new way."

I slowly close my eyes.

Sleep takes a while to come, but it comes.

My body is finding its way to true healing.

It is a few days since the fever broke. I have enough energy to stand up and walk around. Krishna keeps advising me to take it slowly. He chants his favorite Kabir poem when he sees me trying to push myself to go out and fetch water.

'Dheere Dheere Re Mana, Dheere Sub Kucch Hoye

Mali Seenche So Ghara, Ritu Aaye Phal Hoye'

'Slowly, slowly O my mind, in time all things happen.

The gardener may water with a hundred pots, but the fruits happen only in their season.'

Krishna tells me that even this sickness had a purpose for me. I have come to believe him. Krishna tells me that the body speaks the language of the heart. I realize that the fever was the body expelling its toxicity in the way it best knows how. I had survived. The body had survived. The spirit had survived. Healing is happening.

As I have done in the many years before, I am alone with my thoughts. But something feels different now.

All these years, I had experienced my thoughts and rememberings through helpless lenses of self-loathing. Guilt and regret had walked through the walls of my home, and I never once questioned their presence. I had never found the courage to tell them that they had overstayed their invitation.

But my conversation with Krishna has awakened a truth inside.

I had come to realize that all along I had carried a choice.

The choice did not lie in directing the stream of events of my life, though it could have happened. The choice lay in how I was witnessing and experiencing life as it unfolded in front of me with wisdom instead of ego. If I had experienced life through the wisdom of acceptance and not through the lens of self-pity and ego, I realize, I would not have suffered so much. If I had seen myself as part of an unfolding play of life itself, I would not have exaggerated my own role in this drama.

The choice was there before and the choice lay before me now.

I realize I am called to strive, but not to become the striving

To open up to every moment with action that alleviates suffering, but not to identify my self with the outcome of my actions, to accept without question the wisdom of life, without ego, and to enjoy the journey as a gift, as experiences of the heart and not the mind and in so doing live that simple life, without boundaries of imagined fears and experiencing the God within, who knows no boundaries save that joy we call love

I have made choices before. I have suffered.

But all that mattered was this moment.

I feel like a child birthed into a new reality.

This truth would be the end of my suffering.

Chapter Twenty-One

Reflections in the cave: Ego

I am a little envious of this bearded stranger who seems to walk through life with a grace and serenity that I have never been able to experience. Whatever happens, this man seems to accept with gratitude. If freedom from the duality of happiness and sorrow was what Ramdass was seeking with his aghori approach, Krishna seems to have found it more gracefully.

I ask him about this. Krishna seems to be in a good mood for conversation. Perhaps, the ending of winter is elevating his spirit.

"Let me tell you a story that inspired me Arjuna," he says. 'There was a young man named Kaushika who wanted to find enlightenment. For many years he meditated and chanted the holy texts and gained many spiritual powers. His powers inflated his ego and he began to act arrogantly. It took a simple illiterate woman to show Kaushika that he was not on the path of enlightenment. This woman told Kaushika that a truly enlightened man lived in a nearby town, that this person was a butcher, and that Kaushika should learn the secret of enlightenment from him.

Now, as you know, butchering is considered the most despicable of professions by many. How can a butcher, thought Kaushika, a man who takes the lives of animals and sells them, be enlightened?

Still, heeding the words of this woman, Kaushika searched for this enlightened butcher and finally found him. The butcher was not at all surprised to see Kaushika, for he too had gained spiritual gifts. The next day Kaushika followed the butcher around to understand this man's spiritual practice. The butcher had a simple routine. He woke up in the morning, and offered a heartfelt prayer of thanks and surrender to his creator. Then, he went about his everyday tasks, killing animals and selling their flesh. But he did it with a profound sense of karma, with the realization that he was simply a part of a divine dance of life and death, with a complete absence of ego. In the evening, his day done, the butcher offered a prayer of surrender and gratitude and went to bed. Kaushika realized that the butcher had one trait that he did not have, and that was stopping him on the way to enlightenment. It was the absence of ego."

"Is the absence of ego your secret to enlightenment, Krishna?"

Krishna is bemused by my question.

"If I say I have become enlightened, I am not," he laughs. "If I say I have no ego, I have ego."

I smile. I settle for a simpler question.

"What is ego, Krishna?"

"Ego is the illusion that you are separate from the rest of nature. All living creatures aim to exist as part of nature. Only humans desire to conquer nature. Ego tells people

that they are somehow disconnected from the beautiful
mesh of interconnection that nature has organized itself
into. When ego happens, in that moment we believe that
we are separate from nature, we see nature as adversity to
be overcome, rather than the shell that encompasses our
being. What can be more painful and fearful than to be
in constant battle against the ground we stand on and the
very air we breathe? The more we know, the more we seem
to justify our separation from nature. This is the curse of
intelligence. Is intelligence bad? Not at all. But the role of
intelligence should be to bring us closer to nature not to
separate ourselves from it.

When intelligence manifests as ego, it wreaks havoc on
peace.

Ego is what causes us to seek out our differences instead of
our connections. Ego is what causes us to hurt each other,
because it tells us that the suffering of the other is not
our own. In a world without ego, we would learn to live in
harmony with each other and with nature. Perhaps this is
the first lesson we should learn in schools - to tame ego
and coexist with nature. The day ego dissolves, is the day
suffering will cease and peace will happen."

"But are we not all driven to effort because of ego? Would
the end of ego mean the end of striving?"

"I don't think so. Look at the butcher in the story. He saw his
work as an essential part of the functioning of the universe.
He applied himself to his calling and did his tasks with great
love. But he did not see himself as the driver of the drama of
his life. In his mind, there was no drama, no attachment to
outcomes. Here is the truth: Everything that was, is, and will
be in your life is happening precisely as it was meant to be.

To accept this is peace. Sorrow happens when we question this fundamental constraint of truth.

We conflate our own role in the drama of our life. Yes, we draw furrows on the ground, but we don't create the ground. However hard we try, the winds of time blow away the piles of sand we have gathered with our striving. So in the end, we cannot take ourselves or our place on earth too seriously. A kite that has learned to fly with the wind knows the joy of soaring to great heights and experiencing beautiful views."

Chapter Twenty-Two

Spring

Spring has come to Kedarnath.

The mossy brown of the ground has begun to grin through the frosty facade of snow. The sun has come around to unlock frozen pine branches from their glassy prisons. The tinkling of falling icicles and dripping water serenade the growing symphony of birds and insects waking up from their months of winter exile.

The warmth of the sun feels delightful on my skin.

This is a spring that feels like no other. I see and experience the world in the way a blind man might see the world for the very first time. Every smell, every color, every sound resounds with the joy of new beginnings.

My world as I have experienced it has changed in six months.

My heart sings in its newfound freedom- free from shackles of remembrance.

I think the name for this feeling is hope.

It is late April.

Krishna estimates that other shops near the Kedarnath temple must have started to open up for the year.

For a week now we have been getting ready to move back to Krishna's tea shop.

We have packed up the remaining food cans, washed and stacked the vessels, cleaned out the ashes and half-burned wood from the fireplace, washed the blankets and dried them in the sun, covered everything with tarpaulin, and weighed them down with a lining of bricks.

As in the previous years, Krishna would make trips to restock and tend to his cave during the summer months.

Another winter sojourn has come to pass.

We start down for the tea shop early in the morning.

As we board the entrance to the cave with fresh boughs of wood and bramble, the memories and lessons of the past six months come rushing in. I remember the first evening I walked into the cave with Krishna- with one intent- to end my life and escape rebirth. I walk out now with a desire- to live to the best in this current lifetime and recreate my future. All thanks to the healing presence of one kind man that the universe sent as my last lifeline.

Our backs are burdened with all the things that we need to carry back down to the tea shop.

I watch Krishna walk in front of me. He is almost sixty. He walks fast for his age, expertly stepping over the jagged rocks, deftly maneuvering remnants of sleet. He has been on this mountain path so many times that he knows it like the palms of his hands. This cave has been his for many years. A sudden concern sweeps over me.

We stop by a sharp bend of the path to catch our breath. The clouds have cleared and standing on the edge I can see all the way down to the tiny specks of trees in the valley. Suddenly, I am reminded of my smallness and the fleetingness of humans. How tiny our lifespan compared to this mountain, I muse, and how much we make of it.

Krishna's grey beard is fluttering in the wind. He seems to be glowing in the morning sun.

"Krishna," I say softly. "How long do you think you will live this life? The mountain does not grow old, but we humans do. And the path to the cave and back is not easy."

I hesitate.

"I am worried for you."

He is looking at me quizzically, then begins to laugh.

"When I came up this path many years ago," he replies, "I had no idea that this was going to be my winter home. I accepted this opportunity with humility and I made it my joy. I have no idea if I will be coming up this mountain next winter. If it happens that I will be able to do so, it will be a gift. If I cannot, that would be the end of this episode and the beginning of another. Either way, I have no qualms about my eternity. I will enjoy it while it lasts without fear."

"But what if you become sick, just as I did? I had a Krishna to take care of me now. Who will take care of you?"

"Who sent you a Krishna, Arjuna? If the consciousness knows that I need a person to care for me, it will send me that person. When I choose the freedom of acceptance over the fear of safety, I live that much more fully."

I pause to think.

"Perhaps I am the person that the universe has sent your way. I would like to stay here with you, tending to your tea shop, stocking the cave, and spending the winters with you in the mountain. That is, if you are okay with it. I have imposed myself on you heavily so far, but I hope I can be of help going forward."

I look at him expectantly.

He has a distant look on his face.

"Arjuna, I thank you. In the short time you and I have spent together, I have come to love you as a son. Nothing would make me happier than you continuing your journey with me. But I have to say no. This is for two reasons. First I believe you have a destiny bigger than this mountain. You have much to give back to the world. I believe that your years of wandering and your surviving them have a purpose bigger than you. What that purpose is, is for you to find out. But I think it is not to spend the rest of your life making tea with me in these mountains. I could be wrong, but that is what I believe. And..."

He looks deeply into my eyes as he continues,

"... I don't know if you believe in premonition Arjuna. But this year, strange visions have occupied my mind. I have this foreboding thought that I will lose you if you stay here, and I do not want that to happen."

He pauses.

"I hope you understand. I am not making excuses to drive you away."

I do not know what to say. I trust Krishna, but I hope that
he would reconsider.

We take up our baggage and continue our trek down the
mountain toward the Kedarnath temple.

The first visitors have already arrived in Kedarnath. The
temple lights are on and the yellow and red flags on the
temple walls are happily beckoning visitors.

Krishna and I spend the afternoon setting up shop.

I help Krishna clean the shop board, wash the tea cauldrons
and cups that were locked in the tiny inner room of the
shop, which is also Krishna's bedroom, and set up the
frontage of the place. Very soon, Krishna tells me, a supply
of snacks and savories will be arriving from Ukhiamath that
will fill in the tall glass jars lining the front of the shop.
Krishna's tea shop would be ready to operate in a couple
of days.

I spend the night in the back room with Krishna. There
is hardly room for one adult, but somehow we manage to
squeeze in. As Krishna sleeps on the floor next to me, I look
at his peaceful face and thank the universe for him. I tell
myself that if the world got itself rid of the thousands of
fame and money-seeking gurus and godmen and replaced
them with a handful of Krishnas, it would be that much a
happier place. Tears of gratitude flow down my cheeks onto
the towel I am using as a pillow.

Krishna!

Early next morning, I get ready to trek down the mountains. Krishna cooks some food with semolina and spices and packs it for me. He makes tea of course, which we share one last time together. He gives me an envelope with some money that he has saved over time. I refuse. He insists. He tells me that I would need it more than him in the plains below.

At that moment again he reminds me of my mother.

I accept.

"When the time comes, simply pay it forward," he says happily.

Down in Gaurikund, there are buses that connect Kedarnath to the rest of India. They would connect me to all the journeys that lay ahead.

I carry my little cloth bag on my shoulder, now made heavier with Krishna's gifts of clothes and his cassette tapes. And I am no longer dressed in sanyasi garb.

I say goodbye and walk away.

"Arjuna..." I hear Krishna call

I turn back.

"Yes, Krishna?"

Krishna stares at me long and hard.

"Nothing, I just wanted to look at you one more time."

He smiles like the sun breaking through the clouds.

I smile, wave, and walk away.

Something I listened to in Krishna's tapes keeps echoing in my mind in Krishna's voice.

'All rivers must flow to the ocean.

Some rise close to the ocean, some far out.

The ones that start near the ocean -their journey to merge into the vastness is easy.

Some rivers, they are not so lucky. Their journey to the ocean is hard- carving mountains and valleys along the way, braving the hopelessness of not knowing how far away the ocean is, resisting the easy staleness of ceasing to flow, surviving the temptations at every bend to take the easy path out.

All rivers, they must flow. They slow down under the merciless sun, but they do not stop.

In the ceaseless of their flowing, rivers nurture life. Countless come, and call the rivers their home. But the river's own home is the ocean, and this is where she must go.

When the river reaches the ocean, she becomes the ocean.

The ocean gets her wings and floats into the sky.

She falls and hides into the darkness of the land.

She springs forth again with desire and becomes river again.

There is no river, no cloud, no ocean.

Only the playfulness of life.'

I am filled with gratitude for Krishna, the river, who carried a fallen Arjuna to the shore.

'Thank you, thank you, thank you!' I whisper to the universe.

The wind carries my whispers and makes it her own.

News Flash

Disaster at Kedarnath: Thousands of Pilgrims Stranded

Sowmya Mukherjee / TNN / Updated: Jun 21, 2013, 07:57 IST

Three days of torrential rain and flooding have turned
Kedarnath into a ghost town with dead bodies and
debris strewn across the temple town. A massive mid-day
cloudburst led to the melting of the Chorobari glacier and
cresting of the Mandakini river. A landslide happened at
around 7.30 pm on June 16th, followed by flooding that
washed away everything in its path. In the early morning
hours of June 17th, water gushed into the town from
the summit behind the Kedarnath temple, carrying with
it huge amounts of silt, rocks, and boulders. The floods
completely destroyed the town of Kedarnath, which just
a week ago, was experiencing a bustling annual tourist
season.

Intensive rescue and disaster management operations
continue in the area. Since the start of the disaster, the
Indian Army and Airforce have deployed more than 10,000
soldiers and dozens of aircraft to airlift stranded victims
from the region. While thousands of pilgrims have been
airlifted to safe spaces, thousands more are missing or

presumed dead. A senior Uttarakhand government official said 123 bodies have been recovered from Kedarnath. It is anticipated that this number will only increase as teams of experts scout the area.

In what some consider a miracle, a large boulder got trapped behind the Kedarnath temple, diverting the silt and water rushing down from the mountains and protecting the temple from the ravages of the flood. Several people found refuge in the temple as their own homes and shops were flattened by the deluge.

Authorities pointed out that while the temple itself is safe, the silt and debris around the temple were piled to a height of eight to ten feet, and several kilometers of roads had to be restored before people could be allowed back into Kedarnath. The temple is expected to be out of bounds for pilgrims for a year.

Return to Kedarnath

The floods happened 2 months after I left Kedarnath and Krishna.

After a week of incessant rain in mid-June, the mighty Choarabar glacier and the Mandakini river broke banks. Like a petulant child stomping on an anthill, the flood came raging down the mountain, flattening homes and shops, taking away lives and hope. Five thousand either died or were reported lost to the flood.

When I left Kedarnath in April, Krishna had given me a few thousand rupees which he had saved over the years. My protests that he had done more than I would ever be able to pay him back did not matter. Thanks to Krishna's kindness, this madman who had squandered away happiness and sanity now had hope and dreams.

When I reached the plains, I tidied up. A gaunt, bruised, but presentable human emerged from under the layers of grime and matted hair. It is amazing how the body heals after so much abuse. The mind, it takes a little longer. I bought some cheap but decent clothes. I took the train back to Chennai, my hometown.

This time, I did not wander the streets. I had been racking my brain to find friends who would understand. I narrowed in on one. Prashant, my classmate who had given me his betta fish all those years ago, was the one I would reach out to. When I was still in the USA, we had been in touch. He had journeyed through life as an airforce pilot and finally found work as a government census employee in Chennai. I felt he would listen, and that he would not judge. I was right. I found Prashant by walking to the census office and asking for him. It took a while for him to recognize me. It was a time of long embraces and unfettered tears. I had connected with love, I was human again.

Prashant took me into his home without a second thought. After three years of roaming the streets and sleeping out in the open, I found the comfort of closed rooms scary. Even the mundane things- sleeping on a cushioned bed, or using the toilet without having to look over my shoulder, seemed uncomfortable. Reintegration into the old way of living was going to be a work in progress. I would get there.

But there were many gaps that needed to be filled in. The first, and painfully bitter update I received was that my father had passed away two years ago. While I was sleeping on some roadside or temple, my father died alone in his house. I thought of how much regret and pain I must have caused him. I wondered what his dying thoughts would have been. Would he have wept in resentment? Would he have regretted his actions? If only I had not walked away from the house on that fateful night I returned from America...Once again, the could have-beens and should have-beens came ramming at my door. But I had just been through three years of hell walking a very dark path. I was determined not to go down that road again.

Krishna had taught me that to take ownership of anyone's Karma except one's own is folly.

Life is.

Things are.

We strive in our reality, but to think that we direct the course of life with our striving is foolish. What happens happens. When we question this all we are left with is regret. I thought of my father's face and all I could remember was the peaceful face of the dying old man in the hospital. Everything had happened the way it was meant to me. I returned to peace very quickly.

I still was an American citizen. I hoped the US embassy would help me find my bearings. I wanted to return to the US, to tie the human and material loose ends, before returning to India for good. Whether I would find forgiveness from Alice's parents I did not know, but I was determined to try. I would not spend the rest of my life wishing I had not missed opportunities to do the right things. And when I returned to India, I hoped to return some of the kindness I had received. There are many old men dying on the roadsides. There are many Sitas waiting to be rescued.

And so it came to pass that I saw the news about the Kedarnath floods sitting in the lobby of the US consulate in Chennai. My heart sprang in helpless panic as I watched mountainsides and human construction being toppled like matchsticks in the gray deluge. For days the Indian Airforce valiantly worked on search and rescue. All roads to Kedarnath were blocked. Even if Krishna had survived, and had been transported to a different place, I would not know where to look. He did not have any other place except Kedar to call his home. Day after day I looked at the news, scanning the faces of survivors for Krishna. But that piece of relief would never come.

Uncertainty is a painful burden to carry. Sometimes hope fuels uncertainty. As the months passed, something in my consciousness told me that Krishna had moved on. But a secret hope stopped me from coming to terms with this knowing. All this happened when I was still trying to find my way back to the USA. It took me many months and the support of many friends to return to America.

I did not receive the forgiveness of Alice's parents. When I reached their home I found myself facing the end of a rifle barrel. But I did what I had come to do. I begged them, in all earnestness and without ego, for forgiveness for all that had come to pass. And when it was time, I walked away a freer man. A loose end was tied now. I would never be able to change anything that happened. Some wounds, I knew, will never heal. My own healing, I knew, would have to happen by my being a part of the healing of others.

I returned to India. I had a mission to live.

When Kedarnath reopened to the public in May 2014, I was among the first to go. The entire section of the market street leading to the temple had been erased and rebuilt. Krishna's tiny tea shop was no longer on the byroad near the temple. I walked in and out of every shop asking the new owners about my friend. But all of that was in vain. I walked up to our cave, somehow miraculously hoping to see my Krishna walk out from the deeper recesses of the cave. But it was not to be. The cave was intact, but the man who had made it meaningful for me was no longer there. I sat, I remembered, I wept.

The sun was shining bright when I finally walked outside Krishna's cave and out to the edge of the cliff. The clouds floated peacefully below over the great gorge, wafting in the inhale and exhale of the slumbering mountain. For the mountain, the great drama of my existence was no more significant than that of the millions and millions of other livings that called her home. Life comes, life goes, but Kedar, the God of the fields, simply watches bemused.

I feel a tap on my shoulder.

I turn around sharply.

I gasp.

Krishna is standing behind me.

"Krishna!"

Krishna's eyes are twinkling in their usual merry gleam. His gray tousled beard quivers in the wind.

"Are you searching for me Arjuna?" he whispers with the wind. "Don't you know that I am the Universe? Why do you worry about my physical being when I am already a part of you and all that is? Throw away your ragged past and step into your karma, Arjuna. Change lives. Create beauty. Experience love. This will be your offering to life."

I nod my head to the wind.

The beams of the evening sun stream through the branches of the deodar trees.

I brush away the twig that has fallen on my shoulder and start walking toward the plains.

THE END

Made in the USA
Columbia, SC
10 August 2024